All Together Now

ANNIE SEATON

Duckinwilla Days: Book 6

Heartwarming and compelling tales of love, self-discovery, and second chances in the heart of rural Australia.

The Johnson family

Grandmère and Papa: Margot and Robert Johnson

The parents: Hugo and Ellen Johnson

The Johnson siblings:

Charlotte Johnson - Book 1 - *Coming Home*

Julien Johnson -Book 2 - *Secrets and Surprises*

Oliver Johnson - Book 3 – *Wishes and Whispers*

Guy Johnson - Book 4 – *Chasing Dreams*

Amelia Johnson - Book 5 – *New Beginnings*

Lisette Johnson - Book 6 – *All Together Now*

Chapter 1

Charlotte Barrett

The morning light caught the cane fields as Charlotte drove towards the Johnson family farm, turning the waving green stalks into something that shimmered like water in the distance. She'd taken this road thousands of times—first as a child pressed against the back window of Mum and Dad's car, then as a teenager desperate to escape to town, and now as an adult who'd found her way back to the district.

Duckinwilla Valley spread out before her in shades of green and gold, bounded by the purple-blue ranges that seemed to shift colour with the light. It wasn't picture-postcard pretty—this was working country, honest country. Cattle grazed in lush paddocks, and the creek line was marked by the darker green of river gums that had weathered many seasons of drought and flood.

Charlotte slowed the car as she approached the farm gate, noting that the mailbox needed painting and the gate hung slightly askew on its hinges. Small things, the kind of maintenance that could be put off another month, another season, but for some reason, even though they had been that way for years, she noticed them this morning. Maybe it was her news—the secret she carried that made her nostalgic. She pulled her small sedan into the familiar gravel driveway and cut the engine, sitting for a moment to drink in the view she'd woken up to for the first eighteen years of her life. The morning light caught the dew on the cane fields, turning each blade into a tiny prism that threw rainbows across the paddocks. Beyond the cultivation, the Duckinwilla hills rose purple-blue against a sky so clear it hurt to look at directly.

The farmhouse sat in a grove of established trees, its weatherboard walls and tin roof softened by the morning shadows. Smoke rose from the kitchen chimney, and Mum's car was parked in its usual spot beside the back steps.

She parked and sat for a moment, her hands resting on the steering wheel, gathering her courage. Telling her parents about the baby felt like stepping across a threshold into a new version of herself—not just Charlotte the teacher, Charlotte the wife, but Charlotte the mother-to-be, Charlotte the first of the Johnson siblings to carry the family forward into the next generation.

The back door stood open, catching the morning breeze, and the familiar sounds of breakfast cleanup drifted out: dishes clinking, water running, the soft shuffle of her mother's slippers on the kitchen tiles. She climbed the steps and knocked on the door frame out of recent habit before entering.

'Mum? Dad? Anyone home?'

'In the kitchen, love.'

Ellen Johnson stood at the kitchen sink, her hands busy with the washing up, but she turned as Charlotte entered, her face lighting up with the particular smile reserved for unexpected visits from her children.

'This is a lovely surprise. What brings you by so early?'

'I have news.' Charlotte took a breath, feeling the excitement bubble up again. 'Where is everyone?'

'Your father's in the bathroom. I don't know

where the boys are. They ate and went back out.'

Her father appeared in the doorway, drawn by the sound of voices. Hugo Johnson looked every inch the farmer—stained work clothes, calloused hands, and lined face.

'Charlotte.' His voice was quieter than Ellen's but no less warm. 'Didn't expect to see you until the weekend.'

'I couldn't wait until the weekend.' Charlotte moved closer to her parents, her hands unconsciously moving to her still-flat stomach. 'Mum, Dad... Greg and I are having a baby.'

The words hung in the air for a few seconds, then Ellen's face transformed as the tea towel dropped from her hands. She reached for Charlotte, pulling her into a tight hug.

'Oh, sweetheart.' Ellen's voice was thick with tears. 'Oh, my darling girl.'

Dad's face went completely still for a moment, then broke into the widest smile Charlotte had seen from him in months. 'A baby,' he repeated, as if testing the words. 'Charlotte, that's wonderful.' He crossed the kitchen and gathered her into one of his bear hugs, the kind that had made her feel safe and loved her entire life. It was so good to see Dad looking well again.

'How far along?' Ellen asked, pulling back to study Charlotte's face as if the pregnancy might be visible there.

'Eight weeks. We wanted to be sure before we told anyone.' Charlotte wiped her eyes, surprised by her own tears. 'You're the first to know.'

'And you're feeling well? No problems?'

'Tired. A bit queasy in the mornings, but the doctor says everything's perfect.'

'A grandchild,' he said, his voice rough. 'Ellen, we're going to be grandparents. Well, our first official grandchild, anyway.' They all smiled at that. Oliver and Sarah's relationship had brought six-year-old Jett to the family—he called Ellen and Hugo "Grandma" and "Grandpa". He was treated like a biological grandchild by the whole family.

'Your *Grandmère* will be delighted,' Ellen said.

'When?' her father asked.

'October,' Charlotte added. 'Just before harvest.'

'Perfect timing,' Ellen said. 'Oh, Charlotte, I'm so happy for you. For both of you.'

'We're really happy too. Greg and I want to raise him here. In Duckinwilla Creek, I mean. Where family is close by and he can belong.'

'Him?' Ellen raised an eyebrow.

'Or her. We don't care, as long as...' Charlotte stopped, suddenly aware of the fears she hadn't voiced, even to herself. In a world that seemed to change faster each year, where farms struggled and young people left for the cities, would there be anything left of this life to pass on?

'As long as what, love?' Hugo's voice was gentle.

'As long as there's still a place for our children here. A future, I mean. Sometimes I worry that all this—' She gestured towards the window, encompassing the paddocks and the life they represented. '—that it's all disappearing.'

Ellen and Hugo exchanged a strange look. Something passed between them, a glance too quick and subtle for her to catch.

'There'll always be a place for family,' Ellen said finally. 'One way or another.'

Oliver wandered in through the back door. 'I waited outside until the hugs were done. I couldn't help hearing your news when I was about to come in for a cuppa. Congrats, Char.' He came over and kissed her cheek.

'Thank you. And before you ask, yes, we're sure, yes, we're happy, and yes, Greg's already started planning the nursery.'

'October,' Dad said. 'That's...'

'Perfect timing,' Oliver finished. 'Congratulations, sis. Greg must be walking on air.'

'He is. We both are.' Charlotte looked between her father and brother, catching the same oddness she'd heard in her mother's voice. 'Okay, what's going on? You're all acting like October is somehow problematic.'

'Not problematic,' Dad said quickly. 'Just... coincidental. Your mother and I have been discussing some plans of our own, and the timing is interesting.'

'What sort of plans?'

Ellen and Hugo exchanged another look.

'Maybe we should wait until we talk to the whole family,' Ellen suggested.

'Yes,' Dad said.

Unease pricked at Charlotte. 'Talk about what, exactly? You're starting to worry me. Are you both well?'

Dad pulled out a kitchen chair and gestured for her to sit. 'Nothing to worry about, love. Just some decisions your mother and I have been considering. Changes that affect the family.'

'What kind of changes?'

'The kind that needs proper discussion,' Ellen said firmly. 'Charlotte, you've just shared the most wonderful news with us. Let's not complicate it with other things today.'

'But there are other things?' Charlotte pressed. 'Big enough things that you need all of us here to discuss them?'

Another look passed between her parents. Oliver had gone very quiet, focusing intently on his coffee cup.

'Your father's thinking about retirement,' Ellen said finally. 'About what the next phase of our lives might look like.'

'Retirement?' Charlotte's voice came out higher than she'd intended. 'Dad, you're only sixty-two. And the farm—'

'Is a lot of work for a man my age,' Dad interrupted gently. 'Especially after last year's health scare. Your mother and I have been thinking it might be time to consider our options.'

'What options?'

'Maybe we should wait—' Ellen began.

'What options, Dad?'

Hugo sighed and sat down across from his daughter. 'We've been looking at retirement communities. Places designed for people our age, where we wouldn't have to worry about harvests and plantings and could focus on enjoying ourselves.'

Charlotte felt the words hit her like cold water. 'What about the farm?'

'We're exploring that,' Dad said. 'Nothing's decided. That's why we need to talk to everyone.'

'But this is our farm. This is *home*. This is where your first grandchild will grow up and come and visit you.' Charlotte heard her voice rising and fought to control it. 'Dad, you can't seriously be considering selling our family farm.'

'Charlotte,' Oliver said quietly. 'Maybe they have a point. It's a big property to manage. And if Dad's thinking about his health—'

'Don't you start,' Charlotte snapped, rounding on her brother. 'This farm has been in our family for three generations. You and Guy are here to help. *Grandmère* and Papa built this place from nothing. We can't just sell it to strangers.'

'We're not selling it to strangers,' Ellen said. 'We're talking with one company that's made a very generous offer. They want to create a rural residential estate—nice homes on acreage blocks. Another one like where *Grandmère* and Papa live. It would still be a farming area, just smaller holdings.'

'A development company,' Charlotte said with disgust. 'You want to subdivide our farm for McMansions?'

'We have made no decisions nor accepted any offers. We want to secure our retirement,' Dad said firmly. 'And maybe give our children the opportunity to build their own lives without feeling obligated to carry on the family tradition if they don't want to.'

'What if we do want to?' Charlotte demanded. 'What if some of us would like the chance to carry on the family tradition? Did you think to ask us before making plans with developers?'

'That's exactly why we need to have this conversation,' Ellen said. 'To find out what everyone thinks. What everyone wants.'

'Well, I can tell you what I want,' Charlotte said, standing abruptly. 'I want my baby to be able to visit their grandparents at the farm where I grew up. I want them to know their family history, to understand where they come from. I want them to have the same childhood I had— the same connection to the land, and the community, and the traditions that made us who we are.'

The kitchen fell silent except for the ticking of *Grandmère's* carriage clock on the mantelpiece.

'Charlotte,' Dad said gently. 'You live in town. You have a career you love. You've never shown one scrap of interest in the farm.'

'That doesn't mean I don't value what you've built here. That doesn't mean I want to see it destroyed.' Tears pricked her eyes, and she blinked them back angrily. 'I came here this morning to share the happiest news of my life, and instead I find out you're planning to sell your grandchild's heritage to property developers.'

'We're not planning anything,' Ellen insisted. 'We're considering options. There's a difference.'

'Is there? Because you've already been talking to developers. It sounds like you've made up your minds, and now you're just looking for our blessing.'

'That's not true,' Dad said. 'We wouldn't make a decision this big without talking to all of you first.'

'But you'd consider it without talking to us,' Charlotte shot back. 'You'd explore options, and get offers, and make plans, all without asking whether any of us might be interested in keeping the farm in the family.'

Oliver cleared his throat. 'Char, it's not that simple. Running a farm isn't a hobby. It's a business, and it's bloody hard work. If Mum and Dad want to retire, they deserve to retire. They've earned it.'

'I'm not saying they haven't earned retirement,' Charlotte said. 'I'm saying there might be other ways to achieve it without selling to developers.'

'Such as?'

'I don't know. There have to be options that don't involve destroying everything our family's built.'

Ellen and Hugo exchanged another look.

'Maybe there are,' Dad said slowly. 'But they'd require someone in the family to want to take on the responsibility. And the financial risk.'

'Maybe someone can.'

'Do you, Char?' Oliver asked bluntly. 'Do you want to give up teaching and become a full-time farmer? Because that's what it would take.'

Charlotte opened her mouth to answer, then closed it again. The honest answer was that she'd never seriously considered it. Teaching was her passion, her career, her identity. But looking around the kitchen where she'd grown up, thinking about the news she'd come here to share, she wondered whether that was an answer.

'I don't know,' she said finally. 'But I'd like

the chance to think about it. I'd like all of us to have the chance to think about it before you sign contracts with developers.'

'We haven't signed anything,' Ellen said. 'We've only had preliminary discussions.'

'When?'

'When what?'

'When do you need to make a decision? How long do we have to explore alternatives?'

Dad hesitated. 'They want an answer by the end of August.'

'August?' Charlotte stared at him. 'That's only four months away.'

'Which is why we need to have this conversation with everyone soon,' Ellen said. 'Why we need to be realistic about what's possible and what isn't.'

Charlotte sank back into her chair, her earlier excitement completely overshadowed by what her parents were planning. Four months to find an alternative to selling the family farm. Four months to figure out whether any of the family were willing, and financially able, to take on the enormous responsibility of keeping it in the family. Four months to preserve three generations of family history.

'Right,' she said, her teacher voice taking over. 'Then you need to call a family meeting.'

'Charlotte—' Ellen began.

'No, Mum. This is too important to handle casually. If you and Dad are serious about selling, you need to get everyone involved in the discussion.' She stood again, her mind already shifting into planning mode. 'Because this isn't just your decision—it affects all of us. It affects the grandchild I'm carrying and any other grandchildren who might come along.'

'All right,' Dad said quietly. 'A family meeting it is. But Charlotte and Oliver, I want you both to promise me two things.'

'What?' Charlotte had to hold back the pout that threatened.

'Wait until Mum and I get back from Hervey Bay. We're going down there for a few days this week.'

'All right, and what's the second?'

'Promise me you won't get your hopes up about keeping the farm. Don't let emotion override common sense.'

Charlotte looked at Dad, seeing the man

who'd patiently helped with every school project, the man who'd walked her down the aisle. The man who was now talking about walking away from everything Papa had built, and he'd continued.

'I promise to be realistic,' she said. 'If you promise to be open-minded.'

Dad smiled, the first genuine smile she'd seen from him since the conversation began. 'Deal.'

As Charlotte drove back to town twenty minutes later, her thoughts spinning between baby plans and the future of the family farm, she looked at the familiar landscape with new eyes. Not just as the beautiful backdrop to her childhood, but as something precious. Something that could be lost if they weren't careful.

Chapter 2

Lisette

The garden of the wine bar in Fitzroy was exactly the kind of place Lisette Johnson had dreamed about when she was seventeen—exposed brick walls, exposed bulbs casting warm light over reclaimed timber tables, a wine list that required a working knowledge of French regions and Tuscan vineyards. Three years ago, walking into a place like this had felt like she had achieved her dream. Now, surrounded by her Melbourne friends on a Friday night, she felt as though she was watching her life through glass.

'Another bottle?' Chloe signalled the waiter without waiting for consensus. 'We're celebrating, after all. Lisette got that promotion she's been chasing.'

'Assistant curator,' Madison added, raising her glass. 'At one of Melbourne's top galleries. You're basically art royalty now, Liss.'

Lisette managed a smile, accepting the

congratulations that flowed around the table. Six weeks ago, landing the assistant curator position would have felt like vindication—proof that leaving Duckinwilla Creek, leaving her family, leaving everything familiar behind had been worth it. Now it felt hollow, and she had come to a surprising decision.

'You don't look thrilled,' Harper observed, her artist's eye catching what the others missed. 'What's wrong? Is the position not what you expected?'

'The position's fine,' Lisette said carefully. 'It's everything I thought I wanted.'

'Thought?' Chloe pounced on the word like a cat on a mouse. 'Past tense? Liss, this is huge. Do you know how many people would kill for that job?'

Lisette took a sip of her Italian Chianti, wondering what Duckinwilla Creek looked like tonight. Across the garden, Fitzroy's streets filled with noisy Friday night crowds.

'I'm not taking it,' she said quietly.

The table went silent until everyone spoke at once.

'What do you mean you're not taking it?'

Madison's loud voice was sharp. 'Lisette, they offered you assistant curator. At twenty-three. Most people don't get that position until they're thirty.'

'I know.'

'Then why—'

'I'm going home,' Lisette interrupted. 'Back to Duckinwilla Creek. My brother Julien needs someone to manage our family's general store, and I've organised to take over while he and his wife travel for six months.'

Lisette watched her friends' expressions change from shock and confusion to something that looked very much like pity.

'Home,' Chloe repeated slowly, as if testing the word for hidden meanings. 'You mean that tiny town? The one you couldn't wait to escape?'

'The one in the middle of nowhere,' Madison added. 'Where the most exciting thing that happens is the agricultural show.'

'It's not the middle of nowhere,' Lisette said, hearing the defensive edge in her voice and hating it. 'It's a community. A good one.'

Harper leaned forward, her expression genuine concern rather than judgement. 'Lis, is everything okay? Is this about your family? Did something happen?'

'Nothing happened. I just...' Lisette struggled to articulate feelings she'd been processing for months. 'I miss it. I miss home. I miss knowing everyone's name and everyone knowing mine. Who belongs where in the scheme of things. I miss being part of something that matters beyond the next exhibition opening or the right person's opinion. And when I go to the grocery store here, I don't know a soul.'

'But you matter here,' Madison protested. 'Your work at the gallery, your eye for emerging artists—Lisette, you're building a real reputation. And a meaningful career.'

'Reputation for what?' The question came out sharper than she intended. 'To wealthy collectors who treat art like investment portfolios? To artists too pretentious to have normal conversations? To a system that measures personal worth in Instagram followers and gallery column inches?'

'That's the industry,' Chloe said, her tone suggesting Lisette was being deliberately obtuse. 'It's how the art world works.'

'Then maybe I don't want to work in the art world anymore.'

'So, you're going to work in a general store instead.' Madison's laugh held no humour. 'Come on, Lissy. A checkout chick in a grocery store in a country town? After everything you've achieved here?'

'It's not just groceries, and I'll be managing the store,' Lisette said, feeling her temper rise. 'It's a business that's been in my family for three generations. It's a community hub that people depend on. It's—'

'In the boondocks,' Chloe interrupted flatly. 'Let's be honest, Lis. You're giving up a career in one of Melbourne's premier galleries to sell groceries to people who've never left a tiny outback town. That's not romantic or noble. That's just a waste.'

Something cold and hard settled in Lisette's chest. 'A waste?'

'You know what I mean.' Chloe had the grace to look slightly uncomfortable. 'You're talented, Lisette. You have opportunities here that you'll never have back there. You're throwing your potential away.'

'My potential to do what?' Lisette asked. 'Spend the rest of my life curating exhibitions for people who care more about investment returns than actual art? Living in a city where I'm so lonely that I sometimes go entire weekends without a real conversation? Building a life that looks impressive from the outside but feels empty?'

'That's not fair,' Madison said. 'You have us. You have this.' She gestured around the wine bar, encompassing their Friday night ritual, their careful cultivation of urban sophistication.

'Do I?' Lisette looked around the table at faces she'd considered friends, seeing them properly for perhaps the first time. 'When was the last time any of you asked how I was really doing? Not career stuff, not gallery gossip, but actually me?'

Silence again, but this time loaded with discomfort rather than shock.

'I thought so.' Lisette stood up, fishing her wallet from her handbag. 'Look, I appreciate the concern. I do. But I've made my decision. I'm going home, and I'm not apologising for it.'

'You're making a mistake,' Chloe said,

though her tone had softened slightly. 'You're going to regret this.'

'Maybe,' Lisette admitted. 'But at least it'll be my mistake to regret. Not someone else's version of what my life should look like.'

She left cash on the table for her share and walked out into the Fitzroy night, feeling cleansed. Behind her, she could hear her friends' voices rising in discussion—probably dissecting her decision and coming to the conclusion that she'd lost her mind.

Maybe she had. Maybe giving up a prestigious position to manage a general store in a town of six hundred people was crazy. But walking through Melbourne's streets, surrounded by thousands of people and feeling utterly alone, Lisette knew with absolute certainty that leaving was the right path for her.

She'd come to Melbourne at twenty, desperate to prove she was more than just another country girl from a farming family. She'd worked terrible hospitality jobs while studying art history, convinced herself that the exhaustion and isolation were the price of pursuing her dreams. When she'd landed the gallery position, she'd told herself that the hollowness she felt was just imposter syndrome, that eventually she'd feel like she belonged.

But three years later, she still felt like a visitor in her own life. Still felt like she was a stranger to this city. Still felt the ache of missing things she'd been too young and too proud to appreciate when she had them.

Her phone buzzed as she walked towards her rental apartment—a one-bedroom in Carlton that cost more than she could really afford. A message from Julien. **Looking forward to seeing you. We need you here soon. ETA?**

She texted back: **Two weeks.**

We need you here. Four more words that hit harder than they should have. For three years, Lisette had been chasing a life she'd imagined was better than being in her hometown.

But nobody in Melbourne needed her. But home—messy, complicated, imperfect home— needed her. Her family needed her. The store needed her.

Lisette walked the rest of the way to her apartment with growing certainty. The decision had been made weeks ago, really, when Julien had first approached her about managing the store. Tonight's conversation with her friends had just confirmed what she'd already known— she'd outgrown this life. She'd be happier at home than the person she'd been trying to become.

The apartment always looked the same, like a hotel room rather than home. Nothing in it truly belonged to her except the photograph tucked in her bedside drawer—the whole Johnson family at Christmas five years ago, before Charlotte had moved out, before the first cracks had appeared in the family's foundation.

She pulled out her laptop and wrote her resignation letter to the gallery. It was brief and professional, offering the standard two weeks' notice and thanking them for the opportunity. She didn't mention Duckinwilla Creek or the general store or the real reasons she was leaving. They wouldn't understand, and they didn't need to.

She hit send before she could overthink it, before the voice in her head that sounded like Chloe could tell her she was being dramatic, or nostalgic, or foolish.

The following week passed in a blur of packing, paperwork, and increasingly frantic messages from her Melbourne friends trying to talk her out of leaving. The gallery accepted her resignation with professional disappointment. Her landlord found a new tenant within forty-eight hours. Her furniture went back to the rental company. Everything she owned fit into her small sedan.

On Thursday morning, two weeks after the wine bar conversation, Lisette loaded the last box into her car and took a final look at the apartment that had never felt like home. Then she pointed the car north and began the long drive through three states to Duckinwilla Creek.

The landscape changed gradually as she left Melbourne behind—urban sprawl giving way to outer suburbs, suburbs to rural towns, rural towns to open farming country. With each kilometre, Lisette's excitement increased; she was going home to stay.

##

After two long days of driving, Lisette stopped for a late afternoon snack at a bakery in a country town close to home. The woman behind the counter handed her change with a smile.

'Where are you heading to, love?'

'Duckinwilla Creek. Almost home.'

'Oh, you're one of the Johnson girls! I can see it in your face—you've got your mother's eyes. Hugo and Ellen's girl, aren't you?'

'Yes,' Lisette admitted, surprised by how good it felt to be recognised for the first time in three years. That was exactly what she'd been trying to explain to her friends.

'Tell your parents Jean from Aldershot says hello. Your mum and I went to school together.' She handed Lisette an extra lamington. 'On the house. Welcome home, love.'

Welcome home. Two words that made her smile even wider.

Lisette drove the rest of the way with the windows down, letting in the fresh country air. The ranges appeared on the horizon, purple-blue against the afternoon sky, marking the boundary of the Duckinwilla Valley. Her valley. Her home.

She took the familiar turn-off, following roads she'd driven countless times but had convinced herself she'd wanted to leave. Past the Henderson vineyard, along the creek road with its canopy of ancient gums, up the gentle rise that revealed Duckinwilla Creek spread across the valley below.

The town looked exactly as it always had— one main street, shops that closed at five o'clock, people who waved at passing cars even when they didn't recognise the driver. On the corner, their General Store stood surrounded by baskets of hanging flowers.

Lisette pulled into the parking space behind the store, cut the engine, and sat for a moment in the sudden quiet. Through the back window, she could see Julien moving around inside.

She'd left Duckinwilla Creek at eighteen, certain she needed bigger things, more important things, things that couldn't be found in a town where everyone knew your name and your business. She'd spent three years proving she could make it in Melbourne, could be sophisticated and successful and everything a country girl wasn't supposed to be.

But sophistication, she'd learned, could be another word for loneliness. And success meant nothing when you were too far away to share it with anyone who actually cared.

Lisette climbed out of the car, her legs stiff from the long drive, and walked towards the store's back entrance. Through the window, Julien looked up and saw her. His face broke into a grin that reminded her of their childhood; they'd always been close, and she knew they'd both been regarded as the black sheep of the family on various occasions.

Julien opened the door before she could knock, pulling her into a huge hug.

'You actually came,' he said, his voice muffled against her hair.

'I told you I would.' They'd been texting back and forth since she'd told Julien she'd resigned and would help him out.

'I know, but...' Julien pulled back, studying her face. 'I half-expected you to change your mind. Stay in Melbourne where the fancy people are.'

'The fancy people can manage without me,' Lisette replied. 'You can't. Not with you and Emily planning six months in Europe.'

'I still can't believe you actually said yes

when I asked.' Julien shook his head, though he was grinning. 'When I rang you three weeks ago, I expected you to tell me I was mad for thinking you'd give up Melbourne.'

Lisette leaned against the doorframe, remembering that phone call—Julien explaining the Europe trip he and Emily had been planning for years, asking tentatively if there was any chance she might consider coming home to manage the store. 'I'd already been thinking about it. About coming back. You just gave me the excuse I needed.'

'An excuse to abandon a prestigious gallery position for retail in the middle of nowhere?'

'An excuse to stop pretending I was happy.' Lisette met her brother's eyes. 'I wasn't, Julien. I haven't been for a long time.'

His expression softened. 'I wondered. Your emails were always about work, never about you. About friends or relationships or anything that made you happy.'

'Because there wasn't anything making me happy.' The admission hurt, but it was also liberating. 'Just an impressive job title and a lonely apartment and Friday night drinks with people who thought I was insane for wanting to come home.'

'Their loss,' Julien said firmly. 'And speaking of coming home—Lis, about the family. Something's going on with Mum and Dad.

'Yeah, I wondered if everything was okay at home.' Lisette had picked up hints in recent phone calls, tensions in her mother's voice, Dad's unusual silence.

'Maybe that's why we've all been invited for lunch next weekend.'

'Hope Dad's okay.'

Lisette folded her arms. 'Well, I'm here now. For the store, and whatever the family needs.'

'For six months,' Julien said carefully. 'That's what we agreed, right? You manage the store while Emily and I travel, then you reassess?'

Lisette looked past him into the store, seeing the familiar shelves and stock that had been the backdrop to her childhood. She thought about her Melbourne friends, probably gathering for Friday night drinks without her, discussing what a mistake she was making. She thought about the assistant curator position going to someone who'd appreciate it more. She thought about the life she was leaving behind.

And she felt absolutely nothing but relief.

'Actually,' she said slowly, 'I've been thinking about that. What if I stayed longer? What if I stayed for good?'

Julien's eyebrows shot up. 'For good? Lis, you don't have to decide that now—'

'I know I don't have to. But I want to.' Her certainty felt more real than anything she'd felt in Melbourne. 'I'm done with the city, Julien. I'm done with trying to be someone I'm not. I'm staying home, and I'm not apologising for it.'

Julien's grin widened. 'Mum's going to be thrilled. She's been worried about you down there, even if she didn't say.'

'Oh, I knew she was, and I was worried about me too,' Lisette admitted. 'But I'm okay now. Or I will be, once I remember how to fit in here again.'

'You always belonged.' Julien said. 'You just left for a while.'

'And now I'm home, and it feels good.'

Standing in the doorway of the family store, with the valley spreading out behind her and her brother's welcoming smile before her, Lisette finally believed that.

She was home. And this time, she was staying.

Chapter 3

Lisette

Julien had put Lisette straight to work on Monday, and she was restocking the candles and diffusers that seemed to run out of the door when the bell above chimed, announcing another customer. She didn't look up immediately, too focused on arranging the candles by fragrance. Julien had insisted upon that order before he'd left for his morning appointment with the accountant.

'Morning.' The voice was deep and too familiar. Her breath caught, and she turned slowly, already knowing who was behind her. 'Didn't expect to see you back in Duckinwilla.'

Jake Morrison hadn't changed much in the six years since they'd left school—same broad shoulders that came from years of physical work, same sun-weathered face that made it hard to guess his age even though she knew he was the same age as she was, same green eyes that had watched her with barely concealed longing throughout their final year of high school.

'Jake.' She kept her voice even, distant, yet polite. 'What can I help you with?'

'Heard you were managing the store while Julien and Emily swan off to Europe.' He moved closer, that easy confidence she remembered making her stomach flutter in ways that made her cross. 'Didn't believe it at first. Lisette Johnson, back in the valley. Thought you'd decided we weren't good enough for you.'

The barb hit harder than it should have. 'I came back to help out.'

'Right. Help.' Jake picked up a box with a reed diffuser inside, studying the label with more attention than it warranted.

Now, do you actually need a diffuser, or did you just come in to make snide comments about me working here? Perhaps you're here to buy a gift?'

Jake set down the box, his expression shifting to something harder to read. 'Actually, I came to talk to you about the sale.'

'What sale?'

'There are things your parents should know. There's still time to reconsider.'

Lisette frowned. 'I have no idea what you're talking about.'

'Sorry. Forget I spoke.' Jake's rugged face flushed, and she wasn't sure if it was from the heat or embarrassment.

'What *were* you talking about?'

'No, the gossip I heard must have just been that. Gossip.'

Lisette couldn't help herself, and sarcasm laced her voice. 'Duckinwilla hasn't changed then.'

Jake moved closer, close enough that she could smell soap and sun and something distinctly male. 'Was that your excuse for running away? For building a fancy Melbourne life while your family struggled here?'

The accusation stung because it held too much truth. 'I didn't run away. I built a career—'

'In art galleries,' Jake interrupted. 'Selling way overpriced things to people who don't need them. Real meaningful work, Lis.'

'Don't call me that, and it's better than being a stock and station agent who spends his days gossiping about other people's business.'

'I don't gossip. I pay attention. I care. There's a difference.'

They stood nearly toe to toe now, both breathing hard, the air between them charged. This close, she could see the flecks of gold in Jake's green eyes, the faint scar along his jawline that hadn't been there six years ago.

'You have no right—' she started.

'I have every right,' Jake cut her off. 'Because, unlike you, I didn't leave. I stayed. I built a business here, invested in this community, cared about what happens to the families who make it work.'

'You stayed because you had no ambition,' Lisette shot back. 'Because you were too scared to try anything outside your comfortable little world.'

Jake's expression hardened. 'I stayed because I love this place. Because I believe in preserving what matters instead of running away the first time things get difficult.'

'I didn't run away!'

'Didn't you?' His voice had gone quiet, dangerous. 'Because from where I'm standing, that's exactly what you did. You couldn't get out of here fast enough. Couldn't wait to shake off the dust of rural life and become someone more interesting.'

'You don't know anything about why I left.' Jake knew nothing about Brett and the fiasco at the store that had created the rift between her and Charlotte.

'Don't I?' Something flickered across Jake's face, too quick for her to identify. 'Because I remember quite clearly the last conversation we had. The one where you told me you needed to find yourself somewhere that wasn't Duckinwilla.'

Heat flooded Lisette's face. That conversation—their graduation night, Jake's awkward confession of feelings she hadn't been ready to return, her panic-driven response that had been crueller than she'd intended.

'That was a long time ago,' she managed. 'And I didn't leave for ages after that.'

'Some things don't change with time.' Jake stepped back, the distance between them suddenly feeling like a canyon. 'You broke my heart, Lisette. Then you left without looking back. So, forgive me if I'm not thrilled about you waltzing back into town, acting like you care about the district you couldn't wait to escape.'

The honest pain in his voice cut through her anger like a blade. She opened her mouth to respond—to apologise, to explain, to something—but Jake was already moving towards the door.

'For what it's worth,' he said without turning around, 'I hope you figure out what you're running from this time. Because running back to the city won't make it go away.'

The bell chimed as he left, and Lisette stood frozen among the home décor shelves, her heart racing and her hands shaking. Around her, the store suddenly felt claustrophobic, the walls closing in with memories she'd thought she'd left behind.

'Well, that looked intense.'

Lisette jumped, spinning to find Julien emerging from the back office, her expression carefully neutral.

'How long were you there?'

'Long enough.' Julien moved to the counter, beginning his usual morning routine of checking the till. 'Jake Morrison. Haven't seen him this worked up since the council tried to close the saleyards.'

'He's impossible,' Lisette said, but her voice lacked conviction.

'He's passionate,' Julien corrected. 'About this town, about farming, about...' he trailed off meaningfully.

'Don't.' Lisette held up a hand. 'Whatever you're thinking, don't.'

'I'm thinking that Jake's had feelings for you since you were both at school. I'm thinking that watching you come back to town must be complicated for him. And I'm thinking that maybe you're not as indifferent as you're pretending to be. He's still single, you know.'

Lisette wanted to argue, but the words stuck in her throat. Because Julien was right—about all of it. Standing that close to Jake, trading barbs, she'd felt more alive than she had in months. The anger had been real, but underneath it...

'It doesn't matter,' she said finally. 'I'm only here temporarily. I'll probably go back to the city.'

'Is that the plan now?' Julien's tone was gentle but pointed. 'I thought you said you were home for good. But you've changed your mind already because of Jake?'

'I don't know,' she admitted. 'I came back thinking it would be simple. Help out at the store, support the family, all easy. But nothing's simple, is it?'

'Life rarely is,' Julien agreed. 'But that's not always a bad thing.'

Before Lisette could respond, the bell chimed again. She looked up, half-expecting Jake to have returned, but instead found Mrs Grant from the post office, followed closely by old Bill Murphy. Within minutes, the store had filled with the usual morning rush—farmers collecting supplies, retirees buying newspapers, mothers stocking up before the school run.

Lisette threw herself into the work, grateful for the distraction. But throughout the morning, she found her mind wandering back to Jake's accusations. Had she run away? At eighteen, it had felt like expanding her horizons, chasing opportunities, becoming someone beyond the narrow confines of a small town. The issue with Brett that had almost destroyed her relationship with Charlotte hadn't helped either. Now, looking back through the lens of adult experience, she could see the fear that had driven her—fear of being trapped, of becoming powerless.

But maybe, she was starting to realise, she had made a wrong choice.

By lunchtime, her head was pounding. She'd dealt with three delivery men, two supplier disputes, and an irate customer who'd insisted on returning goods that were clearly past their use-by date. When the door finally closed behind the last customer, she sagged against the counter with relief.

'Tough day?' Emily appeared from the back room.

'You could say that.' Lisette gestured vaguely towards the now-empty store. 'A friend of mine from school came by earlier.'

'Something like that.' Lisette studied her brother's face, seeing the strain around his eyes. 'How'd your meeting go?'

'About as well as expected. The store's profitable, but not profitable enough to support both Emily's salary and mine when we come home if we want to maintain current stock levels.' Julien slumped into the chair behind the counter. 'The accountant suggested I consider taking on a partner or expanding the online business.'

'A partner?'

'Someone with capital to invest. Someone who understands retail and could help manage the expansion.' Julien looked at his sister meaningfully. 'Someone with marketing experience and investment in seeing a family business succeed.'

Lisette felt something cold settle in her stomach. 'Julien...'

'Just think about it,' he said quickly. 'You're good at this, Lis. Better than I expected. The locals love seeing you back here, you understand the business, and you care about making it work.'

'I care because it's family,' Lisette protested. 'That doesn't mean I want to keep working here when you get back.'

'What will you do here?'

The question hit harder than it should have.

'I don't know,' she admitted. 'But that doesn't mean the answer is staying here, even if I want to.'

'Doesn't mean it isn't, either.' Julien stood, stretching. 'Just think about it. No pressure, no rush. We've already expanded the store to cater for the tourists. We could add a gallery upstairs. Think about it, Lis. Whatever Jake said to you this morning... he's not wrong about everything. This place matters. And maybe you matter to it more than you realised.'

He disappeared back into the office, leaving Lisette alone with her thoughts and the ghost of Jake Morrison's accusation hanging in the air.

She pulled out her phone, scrolling through messages from her Melbourne friends—updates on projects, gossip, invitations to events she was missing. None of it interested her.

A text notification popped up. Unknown number.

Heard Jake was in the store this morning, hassling you. For what it's worth, he means well. He just doesn't know how to show it without being an arse about it. - Sarah (Oli's partner)

Lisette smiled despite herself. Small-town gossip moved at the speed of light.

She typed back: *How does everyone already*

know about that?

The response came quickly: **Mrs Grant was buying a coffee when he stormed out. She told Bill Murphy, who told his daughter, who told me at the coffee shop. Welcome back to Duckinwilla.**

Lisette laughed, the sound surprising her. There was something comforting about the grapevine, even when it meant zero privacy.

Another message from Sarah: **Also, for the record, Jake's been in love with you since Year 11. Oli told me. Everyone knows it but him. And possibly you.**

Lisette stared at the message, her heart doing something complicated in her chest. She remembered Jake at seventeen—lanky, earnest, following her around like a devoted puppy. She'd been flattered but ultimately dismissive, too focused on her escape plans to see what he was offering.

But the man who'd stood in her store this morning wasn't the boy she remembered. He was confident, passionate, sure of his place in a world she'd spent ages trying to escape. And the way he'd looked at her...

Her phone buzzed again. This time it was Charlotte: **See you Sunday at Grandmères. Everyone has to be there. No excuses.**

Lisette's stomach sank. It sounded very much like Dad had health problems, and no one was talking about it. She was tempted to call Mum, but she knew they were away at the bay this week. Maybe Dad had more medical appointments.

Through the store window, she could see Duckinwilla's main street—quiet in the afternoon heat, unchanged in all the ways that mattered. The bakery where she'd bought hot pies after school. The pub where the whole town gathered for celebrations. The saleyards, where Jake probably spent his teenage years after school.

Jake, who'd loved her at seventeen and apparently never quite gotten over it.

Jake, who'd called her out this morning with brutal honesty about her choices and her running.

Jake, who made her feel more in ten minutes of argument than she had in three years of her "sophisticated" life in Melbourne.

'Oh no,' Lisette said to the empty store. 'This is a terrible idea.'

But even as she said it, she was already thinking about tomorrow's meetings, about whether she could stay in Duckinwilla, about whether six months at the General Store might somehow become permanent. And whether Jake Morrison might be interested in giving her a second chance at something she'd been too young and too scared to appreciate the first time around.

Chapter 4

The following weekend.
Amelia

Grandmère and Papa's house looked like something from a heritage calendar as Daniel and Amelia pulled into the circular drive. Jacaranda trees lined the approach, their lacy fronds blowing gently in the light breeze. The house sat behind established gardens where roses climbed over arbours and citrus trees heavy with winter fruit caught the afternoon sun.

'Looks like we're not the first,' Daniel observed, nodding towards the collection of vehicles already parked in the shade.

'Full house today,' Amelia murmured, though Sunday lunch at *Grandmère* and Papa's was a regular event. What felt different was the urgency in Mum's phone call last week, making sure they would be there.

Grandmère and Papa had built their new mansion in this upmarket housing estate on the edge of town a few years ago. They had moved from *Maison de Rêve*, their first home built in the seventies when they'd handed the cane farm over to Dad, and now where Charlotte and Greg lived.

Daniel parked beside Guy's ute, and Amelia climbed out, straightening the blue sundress she'd chosen because *Grandmère* always expected them to dress for Sunday lunch. The gravel path led through beds of flowering annuals—pansies and primulas in neat rows that spoke of Papa's love of order and *Grandmère*'s eye for colour.

Voices drifted from the back terrace, where Sunday lunch was held when the weather allowed. Soon it would be winter, and the cold afternoon mists would send them inside to the dining room. The sound of laughter mixed with the clink of cutlery and the distant call of magpies in the gum trees beyond the garden. Normal family sounds that made her smile.

'Amelia!' Jett appeared around the corner of the house at full gallop, his six-year-old energy uncontainable as always. '*Grandmère* made pavlova, and she said I can have two pieces if I eat all my salad first.'

'That sounds like an excellent deal,' Amelia replied, scooping him up for a quick hug. 'Are you going to take it?'

'I'm thinking about it. *Grandmère* puts weird purple things in the salad.'

'Those weird purple things are olives.'

Jett pulled a face that showed his thoughts on olives, and then he wriggled down and shot off towards the garden again.

Amelia followed more slowly, taking in the view that never failed to steal her breath. From this elevated position, she could see across the valley to the family farm—the patchwork of paddocks where Oliver was experimenting with different crop rotations, the silver gleam of the new storage sheds, the rusted roof of the farmhouse where she'd grown up. Beyond that, the ranges rolled away toward the coast in layers of blue and purple, each ridge catching the light differently as clouds drifted overhead.

It was a view that showcased everything that Papa and Dad had built, and now Guy and Oli were contributing to the farm.

Amelia's eyes widened when the back door opened and Lisette walked out.

'Oh my God, Lisette!' Amelia crossed the terrace in three quick steps. 'What are you doing here?'

'I've come home,' Lisette accepted Amelia's hug. 'Drove up from Melbourne. Julien's asked me to manage the store while he and Emily travel, so here I am.'

'For six months?'

'Maybe longer.' Lisette's smile was tentative. 'Depends how things go.'

'There you are, Melie.' Charlotte appeared at her elbow, her forehead wrinkled in a frown. 'I was starting to worry you'd changed your mind about coming.'

'I said I'd be here.' Amelia studied her sister's face, noting the tight lines around her eyes. 'What's wrong? You look like someone's died.'

'Nobody's died. But we need to talk, and not just you and me. All of us together.'

'About what?' Lisette asked with a frown.

'About the future. About decisions Mum and Dad have been making without consulting anyone.'

They all turned as *Grandmère* swept out

with serving platters. The long table under the pergola could seat twenty comfortably, and today it held the entire extended family. *Grandmère* and Papa presided from either end, with Ellen and Hugo flanking *Grandmère*, and the siblings spread along both sides. Oliver had Sarah beside him, with Jett bouncing in his chair between them. Guy sat with Elena, their fingers linked on the white tablecloth. Charlotte had positioned herself beside Greg, across from her parents, her expression suggesting she was preparing for some sort of argument. Daniel and Amelia took two of the vacant chairs, and Lisette sat beside them.

'Where's Julien?' Hugo asked, checking his watch. 'He's usually punctual.'

'He texted me ten minutes ago,' Emily said, appearing from the kitchen with the breadsticks. 'He's closing the store at noon and heading straight here. Should be another fifteen minutes.'

'Closing at noon?' Ellen's eyebrows rose. 'On a Sunday? But that's when the coast tourists come through.'

'I know.' Emily looked uncomfortable. 'He said it was important. That he needed to be here for the announcement.'

The word "announcement" made Amelia's stomach tighten as she caught the glance between her parents—something significant passing between them.

They made small talk while waiting for Julien; underneath the casual conversation was an undercurrent.

Julien arrived at quarter past twelve, slightly out of breath and apologetic. 'Sorry, I'm late. Had to finish cashing up and lock everything properly.'

'You closed the store,' Hugo said. 'On a Sunday.'

'I know, Dad. But Char said this was important, and I wanted to be here.' Julien took his seat beside Emily, then looked around the table. 'Plus, I have news of my own. Lisette's home.'

'We can see that,' Guy said dryly. 'She's been helping *Grandmère* for the past hour.'

'No, I mean she's *home* home. She's going to manage the store while Emily and I do our Europe trip. Six months, starting next week.' Julien's grin was infectious. 'Our little sister has come home to mind the family business.'

'Just keeping things running while you're gone,' Lisette said with a smile.

'Six months,' Ellen repeated, her expression transforming. 'Lisette, that's wonderful. But what about your gallery position?'

'I resigned.' Lisette met her mother's eyes steadily. 'It was time, Mum. Melbourne was... it wasn't where I wanted to be anymore.'

Charlotte smiled. Lisette had always been the most adventurous of the siblings, the one who'd taken to city life with the same determination she'd once brought to bossing her siblings around. The idea of her managing the General Store—even temporarily—was going to ruffle a few feathers in Duckinwilla. Yet her time at the art gallery in Melbourne had softened her, and she had become a much kinder person.

'You'll be fine,' Charlotte said. 'You're still tough behind that new soft exterior.'

'Oh, I know that. It's the locals I'm worried about. Some of them still remember me as the mouthy girl who couldn't wait to leave Duckinwilla Creek for the bright lights.'

Grandmère served her legendary roast lamb

while Papa poured wine and kept up a steady stream of commentary about the weather, the cricket scores, and the state of his vegetable garden. The conversation flowed around normal family topics—Sarah's latest jewellery designs, Guy's progress with the new irrigation system, Charlotte's classes at school.

But underneath the casual chat, Amelia could sense strange undercurrents. Elena seemed quieter than usual, limiting herself to brief responses when directly addressed. Oliver kept checking his phone, which was unlike him during family meals. Charlotte barely touched her food, pushing it around her plate while shooting meaningful looks at their parents. Lisette and Julien chatted happily, but Amelia did catch the occasional glance that Julien directed at Dad.

It wasn't until *Grandmère* had cleared the main course and returned with the pavlova that Hugo cleared his throat and addressed the table.

'Before we have dessert, Ellen and I want to share some news with everyone.'

The casual conversation died instantly. Jett continued chattering to Papa about cricket scores, but every adult at the table focused on Hugo.

'Good news or concerning news?' Papa turned away from Jett and asked with the directness that came from eighty-five years of cutting through nonsense.

Hugo smiled, but it didn't reach his eyes. 'That depends on your perspective, I suppose. Ellen and I have been doing a lot of thinking lately about the future. About what we want the next phase of our lives to look like.'

'You're not sick again, are you?' Guy asked sharply. Hugo's heart attacks had shaken the entire family, and despite his complete recovery, any mention of the future triggered protective instincts in his children.

'No, nothing like that. We're both healthy, thank God. But that heart scare made us realise we want to enjoy our retirement years properly. We want to travel, spend time by the ocean, maybe take up some hobbies that don't involve getting up at dawn to check irrigation lines.'

'That sounds very sensible,' *Grandmère* said carefully. 'What sort of retirement are you considering?'

Ellen reached for Hugo's hand. 'We've been looking at Pacific Palms. You know, that lovely over-55s community near Elliott Heads? They have everything—a golf course, a bowling green, and a community centre with activities every day. And it's right on the coast, plus it has a pool.'

'Pacific Palms,' Oliver repeated slowly. 'That's over an hour away.'

'One hour and eight minutes,' Ellen corrected. 'And it's such a beautiful drive. We could come home for visits, and you'd all be welcome to come and stay with us. They have guest cabins too.'

Something cold settled in Amelia's stomach. 'What about the farm?'

The question stayed unanswered for a long moment before Hugo spoke. 'We've decided to sell it.'

If he'd announced he was leaving Ellen, the reaction couldn't have been more stunned. Even Jett stopped talking, sensing the sudden tension among the adults.

'Sell it?' Sarah was the first to find her voice. 'But it's been in your family for generations.'

'Three generations,' Hugo agreed. '*Grandmère* and Papa built it from nothing, I've spent my life working it, and now it's time for someone else to take the land.'

'Someone else,' Guy said, his voice flat. 'Not one of us, you mean?'

'Well, that would depend on whether any of you wanted to take it on,' Ellen replied. 'It's a big responsibility, and farming isn't exactly a secure career these days.'

'Have you asked?' Charlotte's question came out sharper than probably intended. 'Have you asked any of us whether we might be interested in keeping the farm in the family?'

Hugo and Ellen exchanged a look. 'We've been waiting for someone to show interest,' Hugo said. 'None of you has ever expressed any desire to take over the operation. Oli and Guy work particular parts of the farm, but we need to find someone who can afford to buy it because we have to finance our new home.'

'We thought you'd be running it for years yet.' Oliver looked at Sarah. 'We could go and talk to the bank. Maybe?'

'I'm sixty-two, son. My father handed it

over to me when he was fifty-eight. Some might say I've already held on longer than necessary.'

'But you're healthy now,' Guy insisted. 'You love farming. It's your life.'

'It's been my life,' Hugo corrected. 'Now I want to try something different while I'm still young enough to enjoy it.'

Amelia looked around the table at her family's faces, seeing her own shock reflected. This was the farm where they'd all grown up, where Dad had taught them to drive tractors and identify different mangoes by sight. Where Guy had fallen out of the old oak tree and broken his arm, where Charlotte had raised her first calf for the show, and where Oli had conducted his first agricultural experiments in the corner paddock.

'When?' she asked quietly.

'The settlement would be in September,' Ellen replied. 'Which gives us time to sort through everything and make proper arrangements.'

'September?' Charlotte's voice rose. 'That's too soon.'

'It's plenty of time for an orderly transition,' Hugo said. 'We're considering interest from a couple of companies. Maybe for an estate, or maybe selling as a working cane farm. We haven't signed with anyone yet. If Oliver and Guy are interested in staying on as farm managers, I'm sure something could be written into a contract.'

'Stay on as an employee?' Oliver's face had gone very pale. 'On the land I grew up on?'

'It would be good, steady work—'

'I don't want good, steady work,' Oliver interrupted. 'I want to farm our land. *Our* family's land.'

'Son, if you'd ever expressed interest in taking over the farm, we could have had this conversation years ago.'

'I thought my interest was obvious, Dad. I've been working alongside you since I left school. I've been implementing new techniques, upgrading equipment, and improving yields. What did you think that was about?'

Hugo looked genuinely surprised. 'I thought you were helping out until you found your own direction.'

'This *is* my direction. This has always been my *direction*.'

The pain in Oliver's voice cut through Amelia. She looked at her brother—really looked at him—and saw what should have been obvious. The way he talked about soil composition and weather patterns, the pride he took in successful crops, and the care he put into maintaining equipment. Oliver hadn't been marking time on the farm; he'd been preparing to take it over one day. Problem was, Mum and Dad wanted to move, and they needed the farm to sell to finance their retirement.

'What about the rest of us?' Guy asked. 'What if some of us would like to be involved in keeping the farm operational?'

'Are you saying you would?' Ellen asked.

Guy hesitated. 'I'm saying I'd like the opportunity to consider it. We all would, I imagine.'

'Consider what, exactly? Charlotte, you love teaching. Amelia, you're just starting your career at the preschool. Why would any of you want to tie yourselves to the uncertainties of farming?'

'Because it's our family legacy,' Charlotte said fiercely. 'Because some things are more important than career security.'

'Easy to say when you don't have to live with the financial reality,' Hugo replied. 'Farming is hard work, uncertain income, and constant worry about weather and markets and a dozen other factors you can't control. I've protected you children from that reality, but I won't apologise for it.'

'Nobody's asking you to apologise,' Amelia said. 'We're asking you to give us a chance to decide for ourselves whether we want to take on that reality.'

Ellen's expression softened. 'Sweetheart, we're not trying to exclude anyone. But this is a business decision as much as a personal one. The farm needs proper management, significant investment in updated equipment, and someone who understands modern agricultural practices. It's not something you can learn in a few months.'

'And what am I?' Guy's voice was bitter. 'Chopped liver?'

'Oliver understands modern agricultural practices, too,' Sarah interrupted quietly. 'He's been implementing them for years.'

'Oliver's done a wonderful job,' Hugo

agreed. 'But running a farm as an assistant is different from running it as an owner. There's financial responsibility, planning, decision-making—'

'All things Oliver and I have been doing alongside you,' Guy interrupted. 'All things we could continue doing if you gave us the chance.'

Hugo's jaw tightened. 'And if you failed? If the farm went under because you weren't ready for the full responsibility? Then we'd lose the property anyway, plus whatever money we might have made from the sale. At least this way, we can retire and be financially secure.' He turned to Ellen. 'Maybe we're making a mistake.'

His blunt words hung in the air, and Ellen shook her head. 'We're not, Hugo. It's our time.'

Amelia could see the logic, even as she hated it. Farming was unpredictable, and even successful farmers could face devastating losses from drought, disease, or market fluctuations.

But looking around the table at her family, she could also see the cost of Dad's words. Oliver looked like he'd been punched. Guy was staring at his hands, his face drawn. Charlotte sat rigid with barely controlled anger. Lisette was staring out the window, her expression hard to read. Julien hadn't said a word.

'What about *Grandmère* and Papa?' Amelia asked suddenly, the question bursting out of her before she could stop it. 'You can't move away from them either!'

Another silence fell over the table. *Grandmère* and Papa exchanged one of their wordless communication glances, and Papa cleared his throat.

'Actually, we've been having our own discussions about the future,' he said. 'We've decided it's time to move into proper aged care. Sunset Manor has an excellent reputation, and several of our friends are already there.'

'Aged care?' Amelia felt like the ground was shifting beneath her feet. 'But you're both fine. You're healthy and independent—'

'We're in our eighties, sweetheart,' Papa said gently. 'We won't be healthy and independent forever. This place is way too big for us. Better to make the transition while we can still adapt to new surroundings.'

'When?' The word came out as barely a

whisper.

'They have a place available in July,' *Grandmère* replied. 'A lovely two-bedroom unit with its own garden. And a dining room if we want to go there.'

'And activities, and medical care on site,' Papa added.

Amelia looked around the table again, seeing her family's future as very different from what she'd foolishly expected. Not the permanent fixture she'd blithely assumed would continue, but a collection of individuals making choices about their futures. Choices that would take them away from their children and grandchildren.

'I don't understand,' she said, her voice cracking slightly. 'Three months ago, everything was normal. We were all here, the farm was running well, and everyone was so happy. Now suddenly you're all leaving us? *Grandmère*, what about all your furniture, all the antiques? Are you selling them like Dad is selling everything?'

Grandmère drew herself straight, and when Amelia saw the tears in her eyes, she felt awful.

'You don't need to worry. The furniture will stay in the family.'

'We're not leaving you all,' Ellen said quickly. 'We're relocating locally. We'll still be family, still see each other regularly—'

'It won't be the same.' Amelia's words came out flat with certainty. 'Sunday lunches at Pacific Palms won't be the same as Sunday lunches here. Holiday gatherings in aged care won't be the same as Christmas at the farm. Everything that's made us who we are is about to disappear.'

'That's not true,' Hugo began, but Papa held up a hand to stop him.

'Let her finish.'

Amelia took a shaky breath. 'I know I'm the youngest. I know everyone thinks I'm not very practical. But I understand this: if we sell the farm and you move into retirement communities, we stop being the Johnson family and become just people who happen to share a name.'

'Amelia, that's not—' Ellen started.

'I'm not finished. You've made these decisions without consulting us, without considering that some of us might want to fight for what we've built here. You've assumed we'd all be fine with watching our heritage get sold off to strangers.'

'We haven't assumed anything,' Hugo said firmly. 'We've made realistic assessments based on what we need. None of you had shown any interest in taking over the farm.'

'Because we didn't know we needed to show that,' Charlotte said. 'Because we thought the farm would always be here when we were ready for it.'

'Life doesn't wait for you to be ready,' Ellen replied. 'Your father and I have worked hard our entire lives, and we deserve to enjoy our retirement without worrying about the land.'

'Nobody's saying you don't deserve retirement,' Guy said. 'We're saying there might be other ways to achieve it without selling to outsiders.'

'Such as?'

'Family partnerships. Gradual transition plans. Arrangements that let you step back from daily operations while keeping the farm in the family.'

Hugo and Ellen looked at each other.

'It's too late for that,' Hugo said finally.

'We've indicated a verbal agreement to both of the companies.'

The words hit the family at the table like a physical blow. Amelia put her hand on her stomach.

'You've what?' Oliver's voice was barely controlled.

'We have agreed to sell. It's a matter of choosing who to.'

Charlotte's voice rose to nearly a shout. 'You've had this planned and you didn't tell us?'

'We haven't signed a contract yet,' Ellen explained. 'We didn't want to upset everyone unnecessarily.'

'Upset everyone unnecessarily?' Guy repeated. 'You've sold our family farm without telling us, and you're worried about upsetting us unnecessarily?'

'The bottom line, Guy? It's not your farm,' Hugo said firmly. 'It belongs to your mother and me, and it's our decision to make. And it hasn't been sold yet.'

Amelia looked around the table, seeing her siblings' faces set in expressions of shock, hurt, and growing anger.

She looked at *Grandmère* and Papa, seeing resignation and something that might have been sadness.

And she looked out across the valley towards the farm that had shaped every day of her childhood, knowing that in a few months it would belong to strangers.

'Right,' she said quietly, standing up from the table. 'Well, I hope you'll be very happy in Pacific Palms.'

'Amelia, sit down,' Ellen commanded. 'We're not finished discussing this.'

'Yes, we are,' Amelia replied. 'You've made your decision. There's nothing left to discuss. Come on, Daniel.'

She walked away from the table, through the garden where she'd played as a child, past the jacarandas shedding their purple blooms like tears.

Behind her, she could hear voices rising in argument, but she didn't turn back.

There would be time for arguments later. Right now, she needed to drive through the familiar countryside one more time, knowing that everything she saw would soon be lost to them forever.

Chapter 5

Lisette

Lisette pulled into the car park behind the Duckinwilla Creek pub, grateful to escape the oppressive silence of the general store. Her phone buzzed as she walked into the bistro at the local pub. She glanced down at the message on the screen from Marianne.

So sorry! Called in for extra shift at hospital. Emergency in maternity ward. Rain check? Tomorrow night?

Lisette stared at the message, pulling a face as disappointment lodged in her chest. She'd been looking forward to this—catching up with her oldest school friend, someone who'd known her before Melbourne, before she'd tried to become someone else. Someone who might help her remember why coming home had felt like the right decision.

She typed back: **No worries. Hope**

everything's okay. Tomorrow sounds good.

Through the pub windows, she could see the Monday night crowd—mostly locals, a few grey nomads passing through, the usual collection of farmers and tradies finishing their day. Takeaway, then. She'd grab something quick and eat it on one of the picnic tables in the park.

The pub's interior hadn't changed since she'd left—same dark timber, same sporting memorabilia on the walls, same smell of beer and chips and decades of country hospitality. The dining room entrance was to her left, the bar straight ahead, and she was mentally debating between a schnitzel and a burger when she heard her name.

'Lisette?'

Jake Morrison was leaning against the bar, a beer in his hand and a smile that made something flutter in her stomach. Last week, she hadn't noticed how much he'd changed since school— filled out, grown into himself in a way that made her teenage dismissal of him seem even more shallow in retrospect. His dark hair was slightly longer than in those days, his shoulders broader, and the way he held himself spoke of a confidence that hadn't been there at seventeen.

'Jake.' She managed to return his smile, though her heart was doing something complicated in her chest.

'Lis, I owe you an apology. I was out of line the other day.' He moved closer, and she caught the scent of soap.

'No matter. I didn't give it another thought.'

A woman had to keep her pride. Lisette gestured vaguely towards the dining room. 'I was just going to grab some takeaway.'

'Are you meeting someone? I saw you head towards the dining room.'

'I was supposed to meet Marianne, but she got called in to work.' Lisette tried to keep the disappointment from her voice. 'So, takeaway it is.'

Jake studied her for a moment. 'I'm having dinner. I was about to get a table, actually. If you wanted company instead of takeaway...' He trailed off, giving her an out if she needed it.

Lisette hesitated. Having dinner with Jake Morrison—maybe they could make their peace after those harsh words? She'd given a lot of thought since then about how much she must have hurt him on graduation night.

'I'd like that,' she heard herself say. 'If you're sure you don't mind.'

'Wouldn't have offered if I minded.' Jake's smile widened, that boyish charm breaking through his adult composure. 'Come on, I know where the good tables are.'

He led her to a booth in the corner, away from the main flow of traffic but with a view out towards the creek. They ordered—schnitzel for her, steak for him—and settled into the kind of awkward silence that came from not knowing where to start.

'So,' Jake said finally, 'Melbourne. How was it?'

'Lonely,' Lisette replied, surprising herself with the honesty. 'I mean, it was exciting at first. The galleries, the restaurants, the whole city lifestyle I'd been dreaming about. But after a while, it all felt... a bit hollow.'

'Hence the return.'

'Hence the return.' Lisette took a sip of her wine. 'What about you? How do you like working at the stock agency with your dad?'

'Took over the business when I was twenty-one.' Jake's expression sobered slightly. 'Dad had a stroke. Nothing too serious, but enough that he needed to step back. So I stepped up and they moved to the coast.'

'That's young to take on that kind of responsibility.'

'Didn't have much choice. It was either that or sell, and the business had been in the family for thirty years.' He shrugged.

'Hard times, aren't they?' Lisette shook her head with a sad smile. 'I found out what you were talking about last week. I hope our situation can have a happy ending too.'

'The agency is going well,' Jake admitted. 'Really well, actually. We've expanded into three districts, taken on two new agents, and I'm looking at opening another office in Gympie next year.'

'Jake Morrison, successful businessman. Who would have thought?'

'Certainly not you at seventeen.' The words came out without rancour, just a statement of fact that made Lisette wince.

'I was horrible to you,' she said quietly. 'At

graduation. What I said—'

'Was honest,' Jake interrupted. 'Brutally so, but honest. You wanted to leave, explore the world, and become someone different. I was offering you... what? A life in Duckinwilla Creek, running stock sales and living the same life everyone else here lives?'

'You were offering me yourself,' Lisette corrected. 'And I was too young and too stupid to see that as the gift it could be.'

Jake was quiet for a moment, his fingers tracing patterns on his beer glass. 'We were both young and stupid. I was asking you to give up your dreams before you'd had a chance to chase them. That wasn't fair either.'

'Did you hate me? After I left?'

'Hate you?' Jake looked genuinely surprised. 'Like I said the other day, you broke my teenage heart. Spent probably longer than I should have hoping you'd change your mind, come back, realise that Duckinwilla wasn't the prison you seemed to think it was. But hate? Never. And I've grown up since then.'

Their meals arrived, providing a convenient interruption to a conversation that was getting more honest than Lisette had expected. They ate in a comfortable silence for a while.

'Tell me about the gallery where you worked,' Jake said eventually. 'What made you fall in love with art?'

And just like that, they were off—Lisette explaining her fascination with how art captured moments and emotions, Jake describing the satisfaction of matching farmers with the right livestock, the intensity of auctions and negotiations. Their conversation flowed easily, moving from work to family to shared memories of school.

'Remember when Mr Patterson made us partners for that biology project?' Jake asked, laughing. 'You were furious because you thought I'd slack off.'

'You did slack off,' Lisette protested. 'I did all the research while you drew those ridiculous diagrams.'

'Those diagrams got us an A! Patterson said they were the best visual representations he'd ever seen.'

'Because I labelled everything correctly,' Lisette retorted, but she was smiling. 'Though I will admit, your artwork was better than my chicken scratch.'

The evening flew by in a blur of stories and laughter, the stress of the family drama fading into the background. Jake told her about the characters he dealt with at the saleyards, the farmers who still paid in cash, the complicated family dramas that played out over cattle auctions. Lisette shared stories about pretentious gallery openings, the Melbourne art scene's peculiar politics, and the realisation that she'd been trying so hard to fit in somewhere she didn't belong that she'd forgotten where she actually did belong.

'What made you finally decide to come back?' Jake asked as they finished their second round of drinks. 'Besides Julien's Europe trip, I mean.'

Lisette considered the question, wanting to give him the truth he deserved. 'I woke up one morning in my apartment—this perfectly styled, minimalist space that looked like something from a magazine—and realised I'd been there for three years and it still didn't feel like home. I couldn't name my neighbours. I'd spent the previous Friday night at a gallery opening making small talk with people whose names I couldn't remember. And I just thought... what am I doing?'

'And Duckinwilla was the answer?'

'Family was the answer,' Lisette corrected. 'Belonging somewhere was the answer. Duckinwilla just happened to be where both of those things were.'

Jake smiled, something warm in his expression that made Lisette's breath catch. 'For what it's worth, I'm glad you figured that out.'

'Even after how I treated you?'

'Especially after how you treated me. Means you've grown up. Means you're not that scared, seventeen-year-old anymore, desperately trying to prove she's too good for this place.'

'I was never too good for this place,' Lisette said quietly. 'I was just too scared to admit I might not be good enough for anywhere else.'

Jake's expression softened, and he reached across the table to touch her hand briefly.

'You were always good enough, Lis. You just needed to believe it.'

They lingered over coffee, neither wanting

the evening to end, until the pub staff started giving them pointed looks about closing time. Jake paid the bill despite Lisette's protests, and they walked out into the cool evening air together.

'I'm staying in Julien's flat above the store,' Lisette said as they headed towards the car park. 'I can walk from here.'

'I'll walk with you,' Jake offered. 'It's dark, and while Duckinwilla's safe, I'd feel better knowing you got there okay.'

They strolled down the main street, past darkened shopfronts and the occasional house with lights still burning. The town was quiet at this hour, peaceful in a way Melbourne never had been, and Lisette found herself appreciating the stillness.

'This is it,' she said, stopping at the front of the General Store. They stood on the footpath for a moment. The streetlight cast shadows across Jake's face, and Lisette realised with a jolt that she didn't want this evening to end, didn't want to return to the complicated reality of family drama and life decisions.

'Thank you,' she said finally. 'For dinner,

for the company, for not holding a grudge about... well, everything.'

'Nothing to hold a grudge about.' Jake moved closer, his presence warm in the cool night air. 'I meant what I said earlier. I'm glad you're back.'

'To stay?'

He searched her face for a moment, as if trying to determine whether she was being serious. 'To stay?'

Lisette nodded. 'I'm not going back to Melbourne. I'm staying here. In Duckinwilla.'

Something shifted in his expression. He leaned forward, and for a moment, Lisette thought he might kiss her properly. Instead, he pressed his lips gently against her cheek, a gesture that somehow felt more intimate than anything else could have.

'Let's do this again,' he said softly, his breath warm against her skin. 'Dinner, I mean. Properly, not just because your friend cancelled.'

She nodded.

'Good.' Jake stepped back, that confident smile returning. 'I'll call you.'

'I'd like that,' she said with a smile.

'Perfect. I'll call you tomorrow.' He started to walk away, then turned back. 'And, Lisette? Welcome home. Properly home, I mean. Not just visiting.'

She watched him walk down the street, his figure disappearing into the darkness, and couldn't help her happy smile. Then she let herself in the back door and headed up the stairs to the flat.

Alone, Lisette replayed the evening in her mind. What a pleasure it had been. A genuinely good evening, free from family and sibling arguments and the constant pressure to prove herself. And Jake—the boy she'd dismissed so carelessly at seventeen—had grown into a man who was confident, successful, and apparently willing to forgive her for being young and foolish.

Staying in Duckinwilla was becoming more attractive by the hour. She'd come back thinking it was an experiment, a way to see family and figure out her next move. But maybe this was her next move. Maybe home had been waiting for her all along, ready to welcome her back when she was finally ready to stay.

And maybe Jake Morrison was part of that welcome, offering her not just forgiveness for the past but a possibility for the future.

You're getting ahead of yourself, girl. But Lisette smiled in the darkness, thinking of another dinner date and the unexpected second chance.

She'd spent three years in Melbourne searching for something to make her happy.

Turned out, it had been here all along. She'd just needed to come home to find it.

Chapter 6

Guy

Guy pulled into the farm gate just as the morning mist was lifting from the paddocks, the familiar crunch of gravel under his tyres a sound that had marked his homecomings for thirty-three years. But today, even that felt different—everything familiar was already slipping away.

The farmhouse looked smaller somehow, although he knew that was impossible. The weatherboard walls still wore their cream paint, though it was more faded than he remembered, and the tin roof showed more patches of rust that definitely hadn't been there last Christmas. The shrubs by the front steps were heavy with autumn flowers, but even that colour couldn't lift the depression that had settled in him after the family lunch last week.

Family? Huh? What family? He and Elena should have gone to Brazil when they had the chance.

Dad's ute was parked beside the machinery shed, and Guy could see movement inside—probably working on the header again. Dad had been nursing that thing along for three seasons now, and Guy wondered how long it would last.

He found Hugo bent over the engine, grease-stained hands working patiently.

'Morning, Dad.'

Hugo straightened, wiping his hands on a rag that had seen better days. 'Didn't expect to see you back so soon.'

'Thought we should talk. Properly this time.'

Hugo nodded towards the house. 'Your mother's in town. Hair appointment. Coffee's on, though.'

They walked towards the house in comfortable silence, for the first time, Guy noting the small signs of neglect everywhere—the loose board on the front steps, the peeling paint around the window frames, the guttering that sagged slightly on the eastern side. The farm was slowly losing the battle against time and weather.

Inside, Guy stopped short. The kitchen looked... empty. Not literally—the basics were still there—but everything that had made it feel like home was gone. The ceramic canisters that had sat on the bench since he was ten, the ones with the roosters painted on them that Mum had been so proud of, were nowhere to be seen. The collection of tea towels from various country shows that had hung from hooks near the stove had disappeared. Even the old wooden spice rack that Oli had made in his woodworking class at high school was missing.

'Where's...' Guy gestured vaguely around the room.

'Your mother's been sorting out stuff.' Dad's voice was carefully neutral as he poured coffee from the percolator. 'Bit by bit. Some things went to the op shop, some were put aside for your sisters.'

Guy felt something twist in his stomach. 'The rooster canisters?'

'Charlotte wants them for the baby's room. Said something about family history.'

The coffee tasted bitter, though Guy suspected that had more to do with his mood than the brewing. He stood at the kitchen window, looking out over paddocks that rolled away towards the creek line, where cattle grazed peacefully under the climbing sun. It was a view he'd taken for granted his entire life, and now it felt precious in a way that made his chest tight.

'Dad, about the meeting...'

'You don't need to apologise for asking questions.' Hugo sat down heavily at the kitchen table, the same table where Guy had done homework, where they'd discussed school problems and career plans and everything that had seemed important at the time. 'Maybe we should have involved you all from the start.'

'Maybe we should have been paying more attention.' Guy turned from the window. 'I keep thinking about all the signs I missed.'

Hugo's laugh held no humour. 'You were building your own life with Elena. That's what you're supposed to do.'

'But I, especially, should have seen...' Guy gestured towards the stripped-down kitchen. 'When did it get this bad?'

'Gradually. Then all at once.' Hugo stared into his coffee. 'You know how it is with farming. Some years are good, some are tough. We thought we were just riding out a rough patch.'

'How rough?'

Hugo was quiet for a long moment. 'Sit down, son.'

Guy sat, recognising the tone. It was the same one Dad had used when explaining why the dog had to be put down, why they couldn't afford the school trip to the coast, why sometimes adults had to make decisions that nobody wanted to make.

'The drought three years back nearly finished us. Lost a third of the crop, had to sell cattle early when the prices were rubbish. Then last year's flooding wiped out the winter planting.' Hugo's hands wrapped around his coffee mug like it was an anchor. 'We've been borrowing against the land to keep operating. The bank's been patient, but...'

'How much?'

'Nearly two hundred thousand. It doesn't appear in any of the spreadsheets that you were working with.'

The number hit like a physical blow. Guy had known things were tight from his work on the farm spreadsheets, but he hadn't imagined...

'Jesus, Dad.'

'I know. It's a lot.'

'It's not sustainable.'

'No.' Hugo's voice was flat. 'It's not.'

Guy did quick calculations in his head, the kind he'd been doing since the lunch. 'Even if we found a way to turn things around, even if we diversified, went organic, everything we've talked about...'

'The interest alone is fifteen thousand a year.'

'Right.' Guy felt his grand plans crumbling before they'd even properly formed. 'And the over-55s place?'

Hugo's face tightened. 'More than we expected. Good places aren't cheap. And we have to take your grandparents' plans into account too.'

'How much more?'

'Their entry fee's gone up thirty thousand since we first looked. That's on top of the ongoing costs. And because of assets, your grandparents have never been on the aged care pension. The cost of aged care goes up the more assets you have.'

'That sucks.' Guy stared out the window again, watching a crow pick through the short grass near the cattle yards. Everything he'd planned—all their hopeful plans and ambitious schemes—suddenly seemed like children playing pretend.

'There has to be another way,' he said, but even as the words left his mouth, he heard how hollow they sounded.

'Maybe there is.' Hugo leaned back in his chair. 'That's what I keep hoping. That one of you kids will see something I've missed, find an angle I haven't thought of.'

The hope in Dad's voice settled heavily on Guy's shoulders. 'I could talk to the bank,' he said. 'See if there are options for restructuring the debt, maybe a development loan for diversification projects.'

'You think they'd listen?'

'Worth a try.' Guy was already planning the conversation, thinking about business cases and cash flow projections. 'If I could put together a solid proposal, show them a path to profitability...'

Hugo nodded slowly. 'I'd appreciate that.

Even if it doesn't work out, at least we'd know we tried everything.'

They sat in silence for a while, and Guy couldn't stop the memories—breakfast before school, birthday celebrations around this table, late-night conversations during harvest when Dad would come in exhausted but still make time to talk about Guy's day.

'I should get going,' Guy said finally. 'Bank doesn't open until nine, but I want to get my thoughts together first.'

Hugo walked him to the door, and for a moment they stood on the front steps, looking out over the property. The morning was warming up, promising another clear day, and the paddocks stretched away towards the ranges in shades of green and gold.

'Guy,' Hugo said quietly. 'Whatever happens, I want you to know... I'm proud of what we've built. Your input, your life with Elena. Don't let this mess with that.'

Guy felt his throat tighten. 'It's our *family* farm, Dad.'

'It's land. Family's more important than land.'

But driving home, Guy wasn't sure he agreed. The farm wasn't just land—it was his history. It was the creek where he'd learned to swim, the paddocks where he'd learned to drive, the place where every major moment of his life had either started or ended. He was going to have to find a job.

Elena was in the kitchen when he walked into their rental on the other side of the valley, her dark hair caught up in a loose knot as she sorted through paperwork at the table. She looked up at him, and he could read the question in her expression.

'That bad?' she asked.

'Worse.' Guy collapsed into a chair. 'Two hundred thousand in debt. Interest is eating us alive. And the retirement home costs have gone up for *Grandmère* and Papa.'

Elena set down her pen. 'Oh, *amor*.'

'I'm going to talk to the bank. See if there's any way to restructure things, maybe get a development loan.'

'Guy...'

'I know it's a long shot, but maybe if I can show them a solid business plan, projections for organic certification, agritourism...'

'Guy.' Her voice was firmer now. 'Stop.'

'What?'

'Just... stop for a moment. Listen to yourself.'

He looked at her properly then, saw the worry lines around her eyes, the way her shoulders held tension. 'What do you mean?'

'You're talking about taking on more debt to save a business that's already drowning in debt. You're talking about restructuring loans that might not even be possible. And for what?'

'For the family farm.'

'For an idea.' Elena's voice was gentle but implacable. 'For something that might not even be viable anymore.'

'It's viable if we're creative, if we think outside the box—'

'Is it? Really? Or are you so attached to the idea of saving this place that you can't see when it's time to let go?'

Guy felt his temper flare. 'So, your solution is just to give up?'

'My solution is to be realistic about our options.'

'Options like Brazil.'

'Yes.' Elena leaned forward. 'Like Brazil. Where my family has a profitable farm, where they're expanding the operation, where they've offered us a partnership that would set us up for life.'

'And what about my family?'

'What about *mine*?' The question came out sharper than she'd intended, and Elena paused. 'I have parents, too, Guy. I have grandparents who are getting older, cousins I haven't seen in a year because we keep saying we'll visit next year, next year.'

'That's different.'

'How? Because your family's Australian and mine's not? Because your roots matter more than mine?'

'That's not what I meant.'

'Isn't it?' Elena stood up, her papers forgotten. 'Because that's how it sounds. Every time we talk about this, it's about what you'll lose, what your family needs, what this place means to you. But what about what I might gain? What might our children gain?'

'Our children?' Guy stared at her. 'We

haven't even...'

'Talked about it? No, we haven't. Because every conversation about our future gets hijacked by this place, this land, this family crisis that never seems to end. You don't seem to realise that sometimes the farm is all you talk about.'

The words hung between them like a challenge. Guy felt something cold settle in his stomach.

'So, what are you saying?'

Elena was quiet for a long moment, looking out the window towards the ranges. When she spoke, her voice was very quiet.

'I'm saying maybe we made a mistake. Staying here, thinking we could build a life in a place where I'm always going to be the outsider, where your first loyalty will always be to them.'

'That's not true.'

'Isn't it? You're talking about mortgaging our future to save a farm that might not even want to be saved. You're willing to take on debt we can't afford, risk everything we've built, and you haven't even asked what I think about it.'

Guy opened his mouth to protest, then

stopped. Because she was right. He'd been so focused on finding a solution, on being the one to save the family farm, that he hadn't considered what it might cost them.

'El...'

'I love you,' she said simply. 'But I can't compete with three generations of history. And maybe I shouldn't have to.'

She walked out of the room, leaving Guy alone as he realised that trying to save his family farm might cost him everything else he loved.

Chapter 7

The siblings

The coffee shop in Dunmora wasn't as trendy as the one Emily had redesigned at the General Store—cream weatherboard walls that had seen better days, Laminex tables that looked like they belonged in someone's kitchen, and a glass cabinet displaying lamingtons that had probably been there since Tuesday. But it was neutral ground, not in Duckinwilla Creek and far enough from curious eyes and ears.

Amelia arrived first with Daniel, choosing a table on the veranda where they could spread out without the whole room listening in. The coffee was surprisingly good, she had to admit, though her stomach was too knotted to appreciate it properly. Through the window, she could see the main street of Dunmora—wider than Duckinwilla's, lined with established jacarandas that would be spectacular in November. Different from home, but beautiful back-road country.

'They'll come,' Daniel said quietly, reading her fidgeting. 'And when they do, you need to listen as much as you talk. Try, okay?'

She was about to retort when Charlotte walked in with Greg, followed closely by Guy and Elena. Guy looked like he hadn't slept—his usually neat hair was rumpled, and there were shadows under his eyes that made him appear older than his twenty-eight years. Elena moved with her usual grace, her hand resting lightly on Guy's back in a gesture that spoke of quiet support.

They'd barely settled when Oli walked up the steps with Sarah. Sarah's mouth was set in a tight line, and Oli's jaw had that stubborn set Amelia recognised from childhood disputes. Things must be bad if they were arguing; they were both usually so complacent.

Julien and Emily arrived moments later, Julien looking slightly harried. 'Sorry we're late. Had to make sure Katie knew where everything was before we left her in charge.'

'You left Katie minding the store?' Charlotte raised an eyebrow. 'On a Monday morning?'

'She's been working there for two years,' Emily said, settling into a chair. 'She can handle a Monday. Besides, this is important.'

Lisette was the last to arrive, slipping into the remaining seat beside Julien. She looked tired, her face pale, and Amelia wondered if she'd slept any better than the rest of them.

'Right,' Charlotte said once everyone had coffee and the initial awkwardness had settled. 'I know we're all processing the situation, but we need to talk about this properly. Without Mum and Dad commenting.'

'The question is what we can actually do,' Greg said, stirring sugar into his flat white. 'I mean, legally, they're entitled to sell. It's their place.'

'Of course they are,' Sarah agreed. 'But that doesn't mean you can't try to understand why they felt this was their only option.'

Oli nodded. 'Dad looks exhausted. Really exhausted. I keep thinking about how long it's been since I saw him take a proper break. Since he was in hospital last year, I mean.'

'That's what worries me,' Charlotte said. 'What if this decision isn't really about money?

What if they've just... had enough?'

'Can you blame them?' Guy's voice was quiet. 'They're both in their sixties. They've been working that land for nearly forty years.'

Elena leaned forward slightly. 'In Brazil, my parents retired from farming at sixty-five. It's not uncommon. The physical demands...'

'But that's different,' Amelia said, though not aggressively. 'Your family had options. They could sell to neighbours, to other farmers. This is selling to developers.'

Daniel cleared his throat. 'What do we actually know about the offer? The terms, the timeline?'

'Sixty-day settlement, I've heard,' Oli said grimly. 'Though Charlotte, you spoke to Mum after we left—did she say anything else?'

Charlotte shook her head. 'Just that they'd been discussing it for months. The financial advisor suggested after Christmas, apparently.'

'Christmas?' Guy straightened. 'They've been planning this since then and didn't say anything?'

'Maybe they were hoping something would change,' Sarah suggested. 'Maybe they thought they could turn things around.'

'Or maybe they knew we'd react exactly like this,' Amelia said.

Greg winced. 'We haven't handled it well.'

'How were we supposed to handle it?' Oli asked. 'Finding out your family farm is maybe being sold to developers isn't exactly news you prepare for.'

'No, but storming off didn't help either,' Charlotte said gently.

'Enough!' Lisette's voice rose over everyone who was trying to talk at the same time. 'I am ashamed of all of you. What right do we have to put pressure on Mum and Dad? They know what they want, and we have to respect their choice. It doesn't matter if it's another farmer or if it's a developer; it is *their* choice.' She shook her head. 'It's not *our* business, and it's not the town's business. The farm belongs to Mum and Dad, not *us*.'

That made everyone sit back and think. Amelia nodded.

'The real question,' Daniel said slowly, 'is whether there's any way to make the farm viable again. If we could present them with a solid alternative...'

'That's what I keep thinking,' Amelia said. 'There has to be something we're missing. Some angle we haven't considered.'

'Like what?' Guy asked, and for the first time, he sounded genuinely curious rather than defeated.

'Diversification,' Sarah said immediately. 'Agritourism, farm stays, maybe a farm gate shop.'

'Direct marketing,' Oli added. 'Cut out the middleman, sell straight to restaurants and farmers' markets.'

'Value-adding,' Charlotte chimed in. 'Mum's preserves, jams. She's always been brilliant at that.'

The mood at the table shifted. Amelia felt a spark of hope.

'What about organic certification?' Daniel suggested. 'The market's growing, and if they're already using sustainable practices...'

'We are,' Guy said, warming to the topic. 'Dad's been minimal-till farming for years, and he's never been heavy on chemicals.'

'That could work,' Elena said thoughtfully.

'Organic produce commands premium prices.'

'But it takes time,' Sarah pointed out. 'Certification processes, building market relationships...'

'How much time?' Amelia asked.

'Two to three years for full organic certification,' Sarah said. 'Longer to establish reliable market channels.'

The optimism that had been building began to deflate.

'We don't have two to three years,' Oli said quietly.

Guy shook his head slowly. 'We don't, plus there's no guarantee that any of those ideas would work.'

'All good in theory,' Julien said. 'What about the practical side? Start-up costs, cash flow during transition, and ongoing operational expenses?'

'That's the problem,' Guy admitted. 'Even if we could make it work long-term, the initial investment...'

'How much are we talking?' Julien asked.

Guy pulled out his phone, scrolled through some notes. 'For organic certification and basic infrastructure improvements? Probably fifty to seventy thousand. More if we wanted to really diversify.'

Julien was quiet for a moment. 'The store's doing well. I could probably swing twenty, maybe twenty-five as a loan.'

'Really?' Charlotte's face lit up.

'If it meant keeping the farm in the family? Of course.'

Amelia widened her eyes. Maybe she'd been wrong about Julien.

'That's still not enough,' Guy said gently. 'And even if we found the money, there's no guarantee it would work. The market's competitive, and Dad and Mum...' He stopped.

'What about Dad and Mum?' Amelia pressed.

'They're tired, Melie. Really tired. I'm not sure they want to start over with a whole new approach.'

'They might,' Charlotte said hopefully. 'If they knew we were all behind them, supporting them...'

'Or they might feel pressured,' Lisette said quietly. 'Guilty for wanting to retire. They might decide to keep going because of the pressure. And that's not fair.'

'They have a right to retire,' Elena said. 'The question is whether it has to mean losing the farm entirely.'

'What if we took over?' Amelia heard herself saying. 'What if one of us stepped up, ran the place?'

'Who?' Oli asked bluntly. 'You've got your practice. Charlotte is teaching and about to have a baby. Guy's...' He glanced at his brother.

'Guy's what?' Julien asked.

Guy's face had gone red. He stared into his coffee cup like it might provide answers.

'Guy?' Charlotte prompted gently.

'Elena and I have been talking,' he said finally. 'About maybe... exploring other options.'

'What kind of options?' Amelia's voice had gone very quiet.

'Her family farm in Brazil. Coffee and citrus. They've offered...'

The table went silent.

'You're leaving,' Amelia said. It wasn't a question.

'We're thinking of keeping our options open,' Elena said carefully.

'That's the same thing.'

'No, it's not,' Guy said, finally looking up. 'It's being realistic about the fact that maybe there isn't a future for us here.'

'There's always a future if you're willing to fight for it.'

'Is there?' Guy's voice carried an edge now. 'Or are we just being sentimental about something that's already gone?'

'It's not gone. It's our family farm, Guy. Three generations—'

'Of struggle,' he finished. 'Three generations of watching other people's kids leave for the city because there's no work here, no future here.'

'That's not true.'

Amelia felt her temper rising. 'So, your solution is to run away to Brazil?'

'It's not running away,' Elena said, her voice sharp for the first time. 'It's making a life somewhere we can actually succeed.'

'And what about family? What about this family?'

'What about it?' Guy stood up suddenly, his chair scraping against the floor. 'Lisette could up and leave again, Charlotte's in town but talks about Greg's job opportunities at that private school in Brisbane...'

'That's not the same thing as leaving the country,' Amelia snapped.

'Because leaving the country is somehow more abandoning than just leaving?'

'Yes!'

'That's ridiculous.'

'Is it? At least the rest of us are still here, still part of the community—'

'I'm here right now,' Julien said quietly. 'I'm here because this matters to me too.'

Amelia turned on him. 'Are you? Because from where I'm sitting, you got what you wanted—the store, your own business, your independence—and now you're feeling generous enough to throw some money at the problem before you swan off to Europe.'

'That's not fair.'

'Isn't it? You moved away from the farm, Julien. You made your choice.'

'So did you,' he shot back.

'Maybe if you hadn't moved out, you would have seen this coming.'

'That's a low blow. The difference is I still care about the place.'

'And I don't?'

'Do you? Because I don't see you here for harvest, or when Dad needs help with the machinery, or when Dad's in hospital—'

'I was there when he was in hospital.'

'Two days. You were at the farm for two days.'

'Because I have a business to run. Because I have responsibilities—'

'So do we all, but some of us manage to make family a priority.'

Julien's face had gone white. 'You think family isn't a priority for me?'

'I think you like the idea of family more than the reality of it.'

'That's enough,' Charlotte said sharply, but they weren't listening.

'At least I'm not sitting here judging everyone else for the choices they've made,' Julien said.

'What's that supposed to mean?'

'It means you moved out too, Melie. You moved out and built your life with Daniel, like me. But somehow, you've convinced yourself that makes you the family's moral authority.'

'I never said that.'

'You didn't have to. You've been doing that since you were five years old.'

Amelia pushed back from the table. 'I'm trying to save our family farm.'

'No, you're trying to make everyone else feel guilty for not caring as much as you do.'

'Maybe because I'm the only one who does care.'

'Right there,' Julien pointed at her. 'That's exactly what I'm talking about.'

'What?'

'You think you're the only one who cares. You think you're the only one who's hurting about this. But maybe, just maybe, the rest of us care enough to want what's best for Mum and Dad, even if it's not what we want.'

'And you think selling to developers is what's best for them? They said they haven't decided, but they've made a verbal agreement to sell.' Amelia's voice broke.

'I think forty years of struggling and working to keep afloat is enough.'

Around them, the coffee shop had gone quiet; other patrons glanced over at their table.

'I can't believe you just said that,' Amelia whispered.

'It's the truth.'

'It's giving up.'

'It's accepting reality.'

She grabbed her handbag. 'Well, when the rest of you decide you want to fight for something instead of just accepting reality, let me know.'

Daniel stood as well, his face apologetic. 'We should probably...'

'Yeah,' Charlotte said heavily. 'We should all probably cool off.'

As they reached the door, Amelia heard Guy's voice behind them, quiet but carrying. 'Maybe she's right. Maybe we are all just giving up.'

But she was already outside, walking toward the car, and she didn't turn around to answer.

They hadn't moved forward, and now they were meeting with Mum and Dad tonight and pretending everything was hunky-dory.

Chapter 8

Julien

Julien was halfway through unpacking the afternoon delivery when Mrs Patterson shuffled through the door of Johnson's General Store, her walking stick tapping against the polished floorboards. He'd been expecting this. In a town the size of Duckinwilla Creek, news travelled faster than bushfire, and the sale of the Johnson farm was the kind of story that would have tongues wagging from the pub to the post office. Since the meeting with his siblings this morning, he'd been feeling sick.

'Morning, Mrs Patterson,' he called, forcing his voice to sound normal as he hefted another bag of dog food onto the shelf. 'What can I do for you?'

'Oh, just need some of that liniment for my arthritis.' She made her way slowly towards the pharmacy section, but Julien could feel her eyes on him. 'Terrible shame about your family's farm, love.'

There it was. Direct as a hammer blow.

'Yes, well.' Julien kept his focus on the stock, arranging bags with more care than they required. 'These things happen.'

'Forty years your folks have been working that land. Seems a crying shame to see it go to developers.'

Julien's hands stilled on the dog food. 'I'm sorry?'

'The developers. From Brisbane, I heard. Going to put in one of those fancy housing estates, all McMansions and no soul.' Mrs Patterson shook her head sadly. 'Progress, they call it. I call it a bloody shame.'

The liniment tube felt cold in Julien's hands as he passed it over the counter. *Where had she heard about developers*?

'I'm sure my parents have made the best decision they can,' he said carefully. 'And any mention of developers can be taken as town gossip.'

'Oh, I'm not blaming them, love. Economy's been tough on farming families. But it's just sad, you know? All that history, all those memories, turned into fancy houses for city people who don't understand the land.'

Julien handed over her change with shaking hands, grateful when Mrs Patterson finally left. But she was just the beginning.

By ten o'clock, he'd fielded sympathy calls disguised as casual shopping trips from half the town. Mrs Grant from the post office needed stamps but spent twenty minutes lamenting the loss of "real farming families". Old Bill Murphy bought tobacco and launched into a speech about corporate greed destroying rural communities. Even young Sarah Miles, picking up supplies for the school, felt compelled to share her thoughts on urban sprawl.

Each conversation was small, but collectively they were beginning to draw blood. Julien found himself moving stock with unnecessary force, his jaw clenched so tight it was giving him a headache.

The worst part was the assumptions. Everyone seemed to know more about his family's business than he and his siblings did. Everyone had an opinion about what his parents should have done differently, what the family should do now, what it all meant for the future of Duckinwilla.

'You holding up alright?' Emily's voice came from behind him as he aggressively restocked the tinned goods aisle.

'Fine,' he said, not trusting himself to elaborate.

Emily moved closer, her presence warm and steadying in a morning that had felt increasingly surreal. 'Mrs Patterson was in early, wasn't she?'

'Among others.'

'The whole town's talking.'

'I'd noticed.'

Emily touched his arm gently. 'They mean well.'

'Do they?' Julien turned to face her, seeing his own stress reflected in her concerned expression. 'Because it feels like vultures circling.'

'They're worried about what it means for the community. The Johnsons have been part of this town for generations.'

'We still are.' The words came out sharper than he'd intended. 'We're not disappearing. The store's still here. I'm still here.'

'I know that. But the farm...'

'It's just land.'

Emily raised an eyebrow. 'Is it?'

Before Julien could answer, the bell above the door chimed again, and Dave Mitchell from the real estate office walked in. Julien felt his shoulders tense automatically. Dave was one of those men who treated every conversation like a business opportunity, and his presence in the store usually meant he was after information or influence.

'Morning, Julien. Emily.' Dave's smile seemed forced. 'Heard about the farm. Sorry for your family's troubles.'

'Thanks,' Julien said shortly, turning back to his tins.

But Dave wasn't done. He wandered over to the hardware section, picking up items at random while talking. 'Big development planned, from what I hear. Brisbane company, serious money behind them.'

Julien's hands stilled. 'Development?'

'Housing estate. Premium lots, they're calling it. "Duckinwilla Heights" or some such nonsense.' Dave chuckled. 'Bit ironic, given the area's not that high, but marketing departments love their fancy names.'

'Who told you this?'

'Oh, word gets around. I've got contacts in Brisbane, know some of the players in the development game.' Dave set down a packet of screws he'd been examining. 'Funny thing is, they're already talking about stage two. Apparently, your farm's just the beginning. They've got their eye on the Peterson place next door, maybe the Williams block as well.'

Julien felt something cold slide down his spine. 'Stage two?'

'Three hundred houses, they reckon. Shopping centre, maybe a golf course if they can swing the water rights.' Dave's tone was conversational, as if he were discussing the weather. 'Could transform the whole district.'

'Transform it into what?'

'A commuter belt for people who want that country lifestyle but still need to get to surrounding towns for work.' Dave shrugged. 'Good for business, I suppose. All those new residents will need somewhere to shop. It'll be great for the store.'

The tin of tomatoes in Julien's hand suddenly felt heavy as a brick. Without thinking, he set it down with enough force that the sound echoed through the store.

'You know what, Dave?' Julien's voice was low, controlled, but Emily recognised the warning signs. 'Maybe you should take your theories and your contacts and your bloody stage two plans and—'

'Julien.' Emily's voice cut through his building anger like a blade. 'Could you help me with something in the office? Now? Please?'

She didn't wait for an answer, just took his arm and guided him firmly towards the back of the store. Behind them, Dave Mitchell looked bewildered as they walked away.

'I'll be right back,' Emily called over her shoulder. 'Feel free to browse.'

The office was small, barely large enough for a desk and two chairs, but it felt like a sanctuary after the public pressure of the shop floor. Emily closed the door and leaned against it, studying Julien's face.

'Not in public, sweetheart,' she said quietly. 'Whatever you're feeling, whatever you want to say, you can't let them see you lose it.'

'Did you hear what he said?' Julien ran his hands through his hair, disturbing the careful styling he'd maintained since seven that morning. 'Three hundred houses. A shopping centre. They're going to turn the whole district into suburbs.'

'Maybe. Maybe not. Dave Mitchell talks a lot, and half of what he says is speculation.'

'But what if it's true?' Julien slumped into the desk chair, suddenly feeling exhausted. 'What if this isn't just about Mum and Dad retiring? What if it's the beginning of the end for everything?'

Emily perched on the edge of the desk, close enough that he could smell her perfume—something light and floral that reminded him of better mornings. 'Then we'll deal with it when it happens. But right now, you need to stay professional. People are watching how you handle this.'

'I can't believe my parents are selling.' The words came out raw, stripped of the careful control he'd been maintaining all morning. 'I can't believe they're just... pulling up our family roots like they mean nothing.'

'Julien...'

'Three generations, Emily. Three generations of Johnsons working that land, and they're just going to hand it over to some development company so they can build McMansions for people who'll complain about the smell of cattle.'

Emily was quiet for a moment, her fingers playing with the edge of an invoice book. When she spoke, her voice was gentle but firm.

'You've never been interested in the farm.'

'What's that supposed to mean?'

'It means in the four years we've been together, you've visited maybe half a dozen times before we moved here. It means you chose the store over the farm, chose Sydney over Duckinwilla, chose a different life from the one your parents were offering.'

'That doesn't mean I don't care about it.'

'Doesn't it?' Emily's brown eyes were steady, unflinching. 'When was the last time you helped with the harvest? When did you last ask your father how the crops were doing, or whether they needed help with anything?'

Julien opened his mouth to answer, then closed it again. Because she was right, and they both knew it.

'It's where I grew up,' he said finally. 'It's home.'

'No,' Emily said quietly. 'This is home. The store, the town, the life you've built here. The farm is where you came from, but it's not where you chose to stay.'

'That's different.'

'Is it? Because from where I'm sitting, it looks like you want to have it both ways. You want the freedom to build your own life, make your own choices, but you also want everything to stay the same back at the farm, just in case you change your mind.'

The words stung because they held too much truth. Julien had left the farm, chosen the store, built a life that had nothing to do with cattle or crops or the endless cycle of seasons that governed farming. But somewhere in the back of his mind, he'd always assumed it would be there—the safety net of family land, the option to return if city life ever lost its appeal.

'Maybe that sounds harsh,' Emily

continued, 'and maybe you need to grow up now and think about your parents and grandparents. They wouldn't have come to this decision lightly.'

'I know that.' But even as he said it, Julien knew he'd been thinking of the sale as something that had been done to his family, rather than something his family had chosen to do.

'Do you? Because it seems like you're angrier about what this means for you than you are concerned about what drove them to this point.'

Julien stared at the invoices scattered across the desk, seeing but not reading the familiar list of suppliers and stock numbers. Outside the office, he could hear the murmur of voices—customers discussing the morning's events, probably speculating about his family's private business with the casual cruelty of small-town gossip.

'I just...' He stopped, struggling to articulate feelings he hadn't fully acknowledged himself. 'I never thought it would actually end. I thought there would always be time to... I don't know. Go back. Be part of it again.'

'And now there isn't.'

'Now there isn't.'

Emily reached out and took his hand, her fingers warm against his skin. 'I'm sorry. I know this hurts.'

'Does it make me selfish? Wanting to keep something I walked away from?'

'It makes you human.' Emily squeezed his fingers. 'But it also means you need to decide what you're going to do about it. Are you going to fight for something you never really wanted, or are you going to support the family you do have in the choices they need to make?'

Through the office window, Julien could see Dave Mitchell browsing the fishing tackle, probably eavesdropping on conversations and filing away information for future use. Beyond him, the main street of Duckinwilla stretched away towards the ranges, lined with buildings that had weathered decades of economic ups and downs, family dramas, and the slow but constant evolution of rural life.

The town would survive whatever came next. It had survived the closure of the butter factory, the drought that nearly killed the district in the nineties, and the gradual exodus of young people seeking opportunities in the cities. It would survive the loss of one more farming family, even if that family happened to be his own.

The question was whether he would survive it intact, or whether he'd let the grief and anger consume everything else he'd built.

'I should get back out there,' he said finally.

'Professional face?'

'Professional face.'

Emily smiled and leaned down to kiss his forehead. 'That's my boy. And Julien? When you're ready to talk about this properly—really talk, not just rage about developers and family history—I'll be here.'

He squeezed her hand once more before standing up, straightening his shirt, and preparing to face whatever opinions the rest of Duckinwilla had to offer about his family's private decisions. Because Emily was right about one thing—people were watching how he handled this.

And for the first time since his parents' bombshell, Julien found himself wondering if the person he needed to convince wasn't the town, or Dave Mitchell, or even his family.

Maybe the person he needed to convince was himself.

Chapter 9

The siblings

Grandmère's invitation had been exact, as always. 'Two o'clock sharp. Just my grandchildren. No partners today, if you please.' The exclusion of spouses and significant others had ruffled feathers—Amelia had huffed about Daniel being family too, and Charlotte had worried about leaving Greg out of the discussion—but something in their grandmother's tone had brooked no argument.

'She's up to something,' Oli murmured as they waited for someone to answer their knock.

'*Grandmère*'s always up to something,' Charlotte replied, but her voice held affection rather than irritation.

The door opened to reveal their grandmother, impeccably dressed despite the afternoon heat, in a blue floral dress that Amelia remembered from church services and special occasions. *Grandmère* still moved with the grace of a lady.

'Come in, come in,' she said, ushering them through the hallway that smelled of lavender and furniture polish. 'I've prepared tea for later, but first, I have something to tell you.'

They gathered in the sitting room, an elegant space that had always felt like stepping back in time. The furniture was antique but not old-fashioned—carefully maintained pieces that spoke of quality and permanence. *Grandmère* settled into her usual chair, hands folded in her lap with the composure that had intimidated them as children and comforted them as adults.

'I wanted you to hear this from me first,' she began without preamble. 'Papa and I have sold the homestead. We move to Sunset Manor in six weeks.'

The words fell into silence like stones into still water. A chill ran through Amelia. She'd known this was coming—they'd discussed their move at the family lunch—but somehow, she hadn't expected it to happen so quickly.

'Six weeks?' Charlotte's voice was small.

'The buyers are eager to settle, and frankly, so are we. The longer we wait, the harder it becomes.' *Grandmère*'s tone was matter-of-fact, but Amelia caught the slight tremor in her hands.

'How can we help?' Guy asked quietly. Of all of them, he looked the most composed, though Amelia suspected he was still processing yesterday's revelations about the farm's finances.

'I was hoping you might help me pack. Not today—today is for remembering. But in the coming weeks, there will be a great deal to sort through. Many years of accumulation will not fit into a retirement home unit.'

Julien leaned forward. 'Of course we'll help. Whatever you need.'

'Good.' *Grandmère* smiled, the expression transforming her face. 'But as I said, today is for memories. I've been going through some old photographs, and I thought you might enjoy seeing them. Perhaps you can help me decide which ones to keep.'

She reached for a shoebox on the side table—one of several, Amelia noticed—and began pulling out photographs with the careful movements of someone handling precious things.

'Now, where shall we start?' *Grandmère* spread several photos across the coffee table. 'Ah, here's one I think you girls will appreciate.'

Charlotte leaned forward and immediately burst into laughter. 'Oh my God, look at us!'

The photograph showed Amelia and Charlotte at perhaps eight and ten years old, standing knee-deep in the surf at some long-ago beach holiday. They were grinning gap-toothed smiles at the camera, their limbs all angles and knobby knees, hair bleached white by salt and sun.

'We look like scarecrows,' Amelia said, but she was smiling.

'Knock-kneed little things in those dreadful bathers,' *Grandmère* agreed fondly. 'Do you remember that holiday? Caloundra, I think it was. You girls insisted on swimming even though it was winter and the water was freezing.'

'I remember Charlotte getting stung by a bluebottle and screaming the beach down,' Amelia said.

'I remember you telling everyone I was being a baby about it,' Charlotte retorted, but without heat.

'You were being a baby about it.'

'Girls,' *Grandmère* said mildly, but her eyes were twinkling. 'Some things never change.'

She pulled out another photograph, this one showing three boys clustered around what appeared to be a wooden cart with mismatched wheels. Guy, Julien, and Oli, perhaps six, eight, and four respectively, all dirt-streaked and grinning.

'The billy cart!' Oli exclaimed. 'I'd forgotten about that thing.'

'Dad spent weeks building it,' Guy said, taking the photo for a closer look. 'I remember him in the shed every evening after dinner, measuring and cutting and saying "shit" under his breath when the wheels wouldn't align properly.'

'Language, Guy,' *Grandmère* said automatically, though she was smiling.

'It was the fastest thing in the district once he got it right,' Julien added. 'We used to race it down the hill behind the house until Mum banned us after Oli went into the fence.'

'I still have the scar,' Oli said, rolling up his sleeve to show a faint white line on his forearm.

'It's still in the shed, you know,' *Grandmère* said. 'Papa was saying just yesterday that it needs a coat of paint, but otherwise it's perfectly serviceable. Jett could have it now, and then perhaps your baby would like it, Charlotte.'

Charlotte's hand moved unconsciously to her stomach. 'I'd love that. Greg would too—he was telling me just yesterday that he never had anything like that as a kid.'

'What about this one?' *Grandmère* pulled out a larger photograph, this one in colour but faded with age. It showed the entire family gathered around a Christmas tree, three generations in various stages of unwrapping presents and chaos.

'Look how young Mum and Dad look,' Amelia said softly. 'When was this taken? It was before Lisette and I came along.'

'Christmas 1995, I think. Oli was still in nappies, Charlotte was missing her front teeth, and Julien had just gotten that dreadful haircut.'

'It wasn't that bad,' Julien protested, though he was grinning.

'You looked like a pineapple, dear.'

'You still do.' Lisette elbowed Julien.

They spent the next hour going through box after box of photographs, each one triggering stories and arguments and the kind of comfortable bickering that only families can manage. Birthday parties and school plays, sports days and family holidays, the casual documentation of lives lived together.

'Oh, this is wonderful,' *Grandmère* said, pulling out a photograph that made them all lean closer. It showed Papa teaching Guy to milk a cow, both of them concentrating intensely while the cow looked on with bovine patience.

'You were terrified of Bessie,' Julien remembered.

'I was not terrified,' Guy protested. 'I was... cautious.'

'You screamed when she moved her head.'

'She had very large teeth.'

'Still does,' Amelia said. 'Though I think she's about ready for retirement herself.'

The mention of retirement brought a momentary quiet to the group. *Grandmère* seemed to sense the mood change.

'Speaking of retirement,' she said carefully, 'there's something else I wanted to discuss with you. Something Papa and I have decided.'

Amelia felt her stomach tighten. 'What kind of something?'

'We're going back to France. One last visit home.'

The words seemed to echo in the sudden silence. Charlotte was the first to speak, her voice very small.

'For how long?'

'Three months. We'll leave just after we move to Sunset Manor, once we're settled.' *Grandmère*'s hands were steady as she gathered the photographs, but something in her tone suggested this wasn't entirely a happy decision.

'Three months is a long time,' Guy said carefully.

'Yes.' *Grandmère*'s smile was soft but tinged with sadness. 'It will be my last visit home. At my age, such journeys... well, let's just say I want to see my sister once more and visit the places where I grew up.'

Charlotte's eyes were bright with unshed tears. '*Grandmère*...'

'Now, don't start that,' *Grandmère* said briskly. 'This is a good thing. My family still has the old house in Provence, and I have cousins I haven't seen in decades. We want to make peace with our roots before...' She paused, then continued more gently. 'Before it's too late.'

'But you'll come back?' Amelia's voice was tight with something that might have been panic.

'Of course we'll come back. Sunset Manor will be our home. But France... France will always be where I came from. Just as this land will always be where you came from, no matter where life takes you.'

The parallel wasn't lost on any of them. Amelia felt tears pricking at the corners of her eyes and blinked them back stubbornly.

'When do you leave?' Oli asked.

'Two weeks after we move to Sunset Manor. I know it seems rushed, but at our age, these things can't be postponed indefinitely.'

They sat in contemplative silence for a moment, the thought of change settling over them. So much was ending, so much was shifting, and Amelia felt a desperate urge to hold onto something, anything, that would stay the same.

As if reading her thoughts, *Grandmère*

reached over and patted her hand. 'Change isn't always loss, *ma chérie*. Sometimes it's just... transformation.'

'It feels like loss right now,' Charlotte said quietly, her voice thick with emotion.

'I know. But you know what I've learned in my lifetime? The things that truly matter—family, love, the bonds that connect us—those things don't disappear when circumstances change. They just... adapt.'

A soft knock at the front door interrupted the moment, and *Grandmère*'s face brightened. 'Ah, that will be Ellen and Hugo. I invited them for afternoon tea, too.'

She rose with her usual agility. 'Now, let me go and prepare our feast. We're having a proper high tea today—cucumber sandwiches, scones with jam and cream, the works. Consider it a celebration.'

'A celebration of what?' Julien asked.

Grandmère paused in the doorway, her smile encompassing all of them. 'Of family. Of memories. Of the fact that despite everything that's changing, we're all still here, still together.'

As she disappeared towards the kitchen, Amelia heard the front door open and her parents' voices mingling with *Grandmère*'s and Papa's in the hallway. Soon they would all be gathered around the dining table, sharing tea and sandwiches and the careful politeness that had marked their interactions since the announcement of the farm sale.

But for now, in the sitting room filled with photographs and memories, the five Johnson grandchildren sat in comfortable silence, each lost in their own thoughts about the past they were leaving behind and the uncertain future that lay ahead.

Through the window, Amelia could see the sun beginning its descent towards the ranges, painting the valley in shades of gold and amber. It was beautiful, timeless, and for a moment she allowed herself to believe that some things, at least, would never change.

Even if she was wrong.

Chapter 10

Ellen and Hugo

The first letter arrived on a Tuesday morning, handwritten on floral notepaper in the careful script of someone who'd learned penmanship when it mattered. Ellen found it slipped under the farm gate, weighed down with a small stone against the morning breeze.

Dear Ellen and Hugo, it began. *I hope you don't mind me writing, but I felt I had to say something about the news that's been going around town...*

By Thursday, there were seventeen more letters, three delegations of concerned neighbours, and phone calls that started before breakfast and continued well into the evening. The entire district, it seemed, had opinions about the Johnson family's private business decisions.

'Mrs Grant stopped me at the post office yesterday,' Ellen told Hugo as they sat over morning coffee, the latest batch of correspondence spread across the kitchen table. 'She was in tears, Hugo. Actual tears. Said the post office wouldn't be the same without the Johnson farm on her delivery route.'

Hugo picked up one of the letters, scanning the familiar handwriting of their neighbour three properties over. 'Bill Murphy wants to know if we've considered a community buyout. Says he could organise investors.'

'With what money? Half these families are struggling as much as we are.'

'That's not the point.' Hugo set the letter down carefully. 'The point is they care enough to try.'

Ellen studied her husband's face, noting the new lines around his eyes, the way his shoulders seemed to carry more weight each day. 'You're having second thoughts.'

It wasn't a question. After forty years of marriage, she could read his moods like weather patterns.

'Aren't you?'

Ellen looked out the kitchen window towards the creek paddocks, where cattle grazed peacefully in the morning sun. 'Every day. But second thoughts don't change the bank balance, Hugo. They don't make the machinery run better or the seasons more reliable.'

'No,' he agreed quietly. 'But they make it harder to sleep at night.'

The sound of a car in the driveway interrupted their contemplation. Through the window, Ellen could see Guy's familiar blue ute pulling up beside the house. Of all their children, Guy was the one who visited most, the one who still felt comfortable showing up unannounced. He'd visited regularly since he'd started consulting with other cane farms last year.

'Morning,' Guy called as he knocked and entered in the same motion, a habit that had driven Ellen to distraction when he was a teenager but now felt comfortingly familiar. 'Thought I'd stop by on my way to the Hendersons.'

'Coffee's fresh,' Ellen said, automatically reaching for another mug.

But Guy wasn't looking at her. His attention was focused on the letters scattered across the table, the evidence of a community's investment in their family's future.

'More mail?' he asked.

'More opinions,' Hugo corrected wryly. 'Half the district wants to save our farm for us.'

Guy sat down heavily, accepting the coffee Ellen offered. 'Maybe they're onto something.'

'Guy...'

'No, hear me out.' He leaned forward, his expression earnest in a way that reminded Ellen of the little boy who used to bring her injured birds to heal. 'What if there really is another way? What if we're so focused on the problems that we're missing the solutions?'

Ellen and Hugo exchanged glances. This conversation was becoming familiar; variations played out with each of their children over the past weeks.

'You've already been to the bank,' Hugo said gently. 'The numbers don't work, son. Even with best-case scenarios for diversification and organic certification, we'd still be looking at years of debt and uncertainty.'

'But the community support—'

'Is wonderful,' Ellen interrupted. 'But it's not enough to change the fundamentals. We're tired, Guy. Really, bone-deep tired.'

Guy was quiet for a moment, studying their faces. 'When did you know? When did you decide that enough was enough?'

Hugo was quiet for so long that Ellen wondered if he would answer. When he spoke, his voice was very soft.

'Do you remember last winter? During the flooding?'

Guy nodded. The floods had been devastating, wiping out the winter crop and leaving paddocks underwater for weeks.

'I was out checking the cattle one morning, trying to move them to higher ground. The water was rising faster than I'd expected, and I slipped. Went down hard, twisted my knee something awful.' Hugo's hands wrapped around his coffee mug. 'I was lying there in the mud, water rising around me, and for a moment I couldn't get up. For just a moment, I wondered if this was how it would end—Hugo Johnson, found face-down in his own flooded paddock.'

Ellen's breath caught. She hadn't known this part of the story.

'I did get up, of course. Made it to the house, got dry clothes, and finished moving the cattle.

But that moment... that moment when I felt old and helpless and beaten by the land I'd worked for forty years... that's when I knew.'

'Knew what?'

'That I didn't have many more seasons left in me. That maybe it was time to step back before the land took more than I could afford to give.'

Guy's eyes were bright with unshed tears. 'Dad...'

'I'm not telling you this to make you sad, son. I'm telling you because I want you to understand. This isn't about giving up. It's about knowing when to let go.'

'But what about everything you've built? Everything our family has built here?'

Hugo reached across the table and took his son's hand. 'What we've built isn't going anywhere. It's in you kids, in the way we raised you, in the values we passed down. It's in Charlotte's baby, who'll grow up knowing where he came from, even if he never lives here. It's in the way you still stop by for coffee on Thursday mornings because family matters more than convenience.'

'It won't be the same without the farm.'

'No,' Hugo agreed. 'It won't be the same. But different doesn't always mean worse, Guy. Sometimes it just means different.'

Ellen watched her husband and son, seeing so much of Hugo in Guy's earnest expression, in the way he wrestled with concepts too large for simple answers. Of all their children, Guy had inherited Hugo's deep connection to the land, his instinctive understanding of weather patterns and soil conditions and the intricate dance between human effort and natural forces.

'I keep thinking about Papa and then you, Dad,' Guy said suddenly. 'About what you both went through, from clearing the land to building it up to what it was in the good times. Because Dad, nothing you've done has caused this situation. We know it's the uncertainty of being on the land, at the mercy of nature and the banks.'

Hugo's grip on Guy's hand tightened. 'Your grandfather was twenty-three when he arrived back in Australia,' he said. 'Twenty-three, with a pregnant wife.'

Guy's voice was thick with emotion. 'We know he built this place from nothing, Dad.

Cleared the land by hand, built the first house with timber he cut himself. How do we just... walk away from that?'

'We don't walk away from it,' Hugo said quietly. 'We honour it by making the hard choices he would have made. Papa didn't hold onto things that weren't working. He adapted, he changed, he did whatever it took to provide for his family.'

'But he never gave up.'

'He didn't?' Hugo's voice was gentle but firm.

Guy brushed away the tears that were threatening. 'I don't want to lose this place.'

'Neither do I.' Hugo's own voice was breaking. 'God help me, neither do I. But I can't keep it just because letting go hurts. I can't sacrifice your mother's health, your grandparents' comfort, our family's financial security, just because I'm too stubborn or too proud to admit when I'm beaten.'

'You're not beaten, Dad. You're tired. There's a difference.'

'Is there?' Hugo wiped his eyes with the back of his free hand. 'Because some days I can't tell anymore.'

Ellen felt her own tears starting, watching these two men she loved struggle with forces larger than any individual will. She started to rise, to offer comfort or distraction or simple presence, but something stopped her.

This wasn't her conversation to interrupt. This was father and son, working through grief and acceptance. This was the passing of something that couldn't be passed, the acknowledgement that some burdens were too heavy for the next generation to carry.

'I love you, Dad,' Guy said simply.

'I love you too, son. That's why I have to let go.'

They sat in silence for a moment, hands clasped across the kitchen table. Outside, the morning was building towards noon, the sun climbing higher over the cane.

Ellen was about to speak when she heard footsteps on the front veranda, then the familiar sound of the door opening. 'Hugo? Are you in the kitchen?'

Grandmère's voice, calling from the hallway. Ellen started to respond, but her voice caught when she saw the two men at her table, still holding hands, both with tears on their faces and expressions too raw for public consumption.

The footsteps approached the kitchen doorway and then stopped. Ellen could picture her mother-in-law taking in the scene—Hugo and Guy, caught in a moment of pure vulnerability, processing grief too large for easy words.

The footsteps retreated quietly, and Ellen heard the soft click of the front door closing. *Grandmère*, with the wisdom of eight decades, understanding when to give privacy to pain.

'She's gone,' Ellen said softly.

Hugo nodded, finally releasing Guy's hand and reaching for a tea towel to wipe his face. 'Your grandmother has always known when to leave people alone with their feelings.'

'Unlike the rest of the district,' Guy said, managing a watery smile as he gestured towards the pile of letters.

'The district means well,' Ellen said. 'They're just scared. Scared of losing something that feels permanent in a world where nothing else does.'

'Are we doing the right thing?' Guy asked, and Ellen heard in his voice the little boy who used to ask the same question about everything from school projects to injured animals.

'We're doing the only thing we can do,' Hugo answered. 'Whether it's right or wrong... well, I suppose we'll find out.'

Outside, a crow called from the direction of the creek, and Ellen held the sound, filing it away with all the other small details that made this place home. Because whatever came next, whatever decisions were made or unmade, this kitchen conversation would be one of the last before everything changed.

And that, she realised, was something worth remembering.

Chapter 11

The family

The family meeting was scheduled for six o'clock, but Lisette arrived at the farm at five. Mum was in the kitchen, as she'd known she would be, preparing enough food to feed twice the number of people who'd be there.

'You're early,' Ellen said, not looking up from the salads she was making.

'Thought you might need help.' Lisette washed her hands and began slicing tomatoes from habit.

They worked in companionable silence for a while, the only sounds the knife against the cutting board and the soft hum of the refrigerator. Outside, the afternoon was fading into evening, painting the paddocks in shades of amber and gold.

'Jake Morrison and I had dinner again last night,' Lisette said finally.

Ellen's hands stilled briefly before resuming

their work. 'And?'

'He had opinions about the farm sale.'

'Jake has opinions about everything.' Ellen's tone was neutral, carefully so. 'Always has, even as a boy. His father was the same—passionate about the district, protective of the old ways.'

'He thinks we're betraying *Grandmère* and Papa's legacy.'

'He's not the only one.' Ellen set down her knife and looked at her daughter properly. 'Lisette, I need you to understand something. Your father and I didn't make this decision lightly. We've thought about it from every angle, considered every alternative. When you first heard, you thought we were selling out. Running away from responsibility.'

'Maybe,' Lisette admitted. 'But that was before I understood how tired you both are. Before I saw the stripped-down kitchen and the letters from neighbours and the worry Dad's been carrying.'

Ellen's eyes glistened with unshed tears. 'We wanted to protect you children from all of that. From the financial pressures and the endless worry and the knowledge that sometimes love isn't enough to keep something alive.'

'I'm not a child anymore, Mum.'

'No.' Ellen managed a watery smile. 'No, you're not. And maybe that's part of why this is so hard. Watching you all process this as adults, with adult perspectives and adult stake in the outcome. It was easier when you were young and we could make decisions without explaining them.'

The sound of vehicles at the back of the house announced the arrival of the rest of the family. Through the kitchen window, Lisette watched Charlotte and Greg walk across the back lawn, followed by Guy and Elena, then Amelia and Daniel. Oli and Sarah arrived last, with Jett bouncing between them. Julien and Emily had arrived not long after Lisette when they locked up the store.

Within minutes, the house filled with the usual chaos of a Johnson family get-together. But this wasn't a birthday or a family dinner, and Lisette could feel the tension.

They gathered in the living room; Hugo stood by the window, his expression set, while

Ellen hovered in the kitchen doorway.

'Right,' Charlotte said, taking charge with her teacher's voice. 'We're all here. Let's talk about where things stand.'

'Where things stand is still that we're selling,' Hugo said bluntly. 'That hasn't changed.'

'But maybe it should,' Amelia interjected. 'Mum, Dad, the whole community is rallying around us. There are letters, offers of help, people willing to invest—'

'People willing to throw good money after bad,' Hugo corrected. 'Amelia, I appreciate the sentiment. But this isn't a fairy tale where what a community wants magically solves financial problems.'

'It's not magic, it's practical alternatives,' Oli said. 'I've been working with the bank, Dad. There are restructuring options—'

'That would still leave us in debt,' Hugo finished. 'For years. Possibly decades. And for what? So we can work ourselves to death maintaining a property none of you want to run?'

'*I* want to run it,' Oli said quietly.

The room went silent. Ellen's hand flew to

her mouth, and Hugo's eyebrows rose.

'What?' he managed finally.

'I want to run the farm,' Oli repeated, louder this time. 'I've always wanted to. I thought you knew that.'

'But your work with the Hendersons and—'

'Is contract work. It's helping out neighbours, learning new techniques, but it's not what I want long-term.' Oli stood up, his hands clenched at his sides. 'I want to farm *our* land, Dad. I want to build on what you and *Grandmère,* and Papa created. I want Jett to grow up here, learning about seasons and soil and the satisfaction that comes from growing things.'

Sarah reached for his hand. 'We've talked about this,' she added quietly. 'For months. We were waiting for the right time to tell you, and then you announced the sale, and everything got complicated.'

Hugo stood there, shock on his face. 'You never said anything.'

'Because I thought you knew,' Oli's voice cracked slightly. 'I thought it was obvious. I've been working alongside you and Guy for years, implementing new systems, upgrading equipment, and talking about long-term sustainability. What did you think that was about?'

'I thought you were helping out until you found your own direction.'

'This is my direction,' Oli said fiercely. 'This has always been my direction. The farm is my direction.'

Beside Lisette, Guy shifted uncomfortably, and she realised her brother had known—had probably guessed months ago what Oli wanted but hadn't said anything because the Johnson boys had never been good at communicating.

'Even if you want it,' Hugo said, shaking his head, 'that doesn't change the finances. The debt is still there. The equipment still needs replacing. The challenges that made us decide to sell don't disappear just because you're willing to take them on.'

'But they become my challenges,' Oli argued. 'My risk, my responsibility. You and Mum can still retire, move to the coast, and still have the life you want. But the farm stays in the family.'

'With what money?' Ellen asked practically.

'Oli, buying us out would require capital you don't have. The bank won't loan you enough to cover both the purchase price and the operational debt.'

'What if we all went in together?' Julien said suddenly. Everyone turned to look at him. 'What if it wasn't just Oli? What if it was a family partnership?'

'You want to farm here too?' Hugo asked incredulously.

'No, but we all want the farm to stay in the family.' Julien pulled out his phone, scrolling through notes. 'I've been doing some research. If we formed a family trust, with Oli as the primary operator and the rest of us as investors, we could potentially raise enough capital to buy you out and cover the operational debt.'

'That's wishful thinking,' Hugo said.

'Is it?' Julien leaned forward. 'Because I've been looking at similar structures across family-owned stores. Oli's right—there are legal frameworks that would let us pool resources while limiting individual risk.'

'I could invest,' Amelia added. 'Not a huge amount, but something.'

'Greg and I have savings,' Charlotte said. 'For the baby, for the house, but if keeping the farm means that much—'

'No,' Ellen said firmly. 'Absolutely not. We are not taking money from our children's futures to prop up a failing business.'

'It's not failing if we run it properly,' Oli insisted. 'Mum, the farm isn't failing because of bad management or lack of effort. It's struggling because of circumstances outside anyone's control—drought, flooding, market conditions. Those things change. With the right approach, diversification, modern techniques—'

'It's still a gamble,' Hugo said. 'A huge gamble with your siblings' money.'

'Then let us decide if we want to take that gamble,' Julien said. 'Dad, you and Mum have spent forty years making decisions about this farm. Maybe it's time to let the next generation make some decisions too.'

Hugo looked at Ellen, wordless communication passing between them. Lisette could see her father wavering, indecision, but hope, in his expression.

'What about you?' Amelia asked suddenly,

looking at Lisette. 'You've been quiet. What do you think?'

All eyes turned to her. Lisette's throat tightened, aware that whatever she said next was important.

'I think,' she said carefully, 'that the farm matters. To all of us, but especially to Oli. And I think maybe some things are worth fighting for, even when it's scary and uncertain.'

'That's easy to say when you're not the one taking the financial risk,' Guy pointed out, not unkindly.

'I know. But what if I was?' The words were out before Lisette fully realised what she was saying. 'What if I stay? What if I become Julien's partner in the store and invest my savings in the family trust? I was on a very good salary in Melbourne.'

Silence filled the room. Oli's face lit up with hope. Ellen looked shocked, and Charlotte reached for her hand.

'But what about Melbourne?' Hugo asked quietly, cutting through the noise. 'You're definitely not going back?'

'I'm not,' Lisette replied.

'Are you really sure?' Amelia's question wasn't accusatory, just genuinely curious.

'Yes, I am. Since I came back and realised what I was missing.' Lisette thought about Jake's accusation, about running away, about three years of building a life that looked impressive from the outside but felt increasingly empty from within. 'I thought leaving Duckinwilla meant growing up, becoming someone important in a more important place. But maybe growing up means understanding where you really belong.'

'And you belong here?' Ellen's voice was thick with emotion.

'I think I might.' Lisette smiled at her mother. 'If you'll have me.'

Hugo reached for Ellen's hand, and their gazes met and held. 'Right,' he said. 'I'm going to play devil's advocate. Let's talk this over.'

The discussion that followed was intense, practical, and focused on dollars, percentages, land values, and legal structures. Julien provided explanations of trust arrangements and investment frameworks. Oli outlined his vision for the farm's future—organic certification, agritourism, and direct marketing to restaurants.

Charlotte talked about educational programs and school partnerships. Even Jett contributed an idea about having a farm nursery for people to visit.

Through it all, Hugo and Ellen listened, and Lisette could see acceptance gradually building.

'It's not a decision we can make tonight,' Hugo said finally, when the discussion had exhausted itself. 'Your mum and I need time to think, to get financial advice, and really think about what you're all proposing.'

'But you'll consider it?' Oli asked, and Lisette heard the boy he'd once been in his voice—hopeful, eager, needing approval from Dad.

'We'll consider it,' Hugo confirmed. 'That's all I can promise right now.'

It was enough. The relief in the room was palpable as the conversation shifted to lighter topics—Jett's upcoming birthday, Charlotte's nursery plans, Lisette's enjoyment of working at the store. The barbeque was lit, and Mum's salads brought out, and for a while, they were a family again, laughing and arguing as they always had.

Lisette was helping clear the table on the back veranda when she heard a knock at the front door. Ellen went to answer it, and Lisette's stomach dropped when Mum led Jake through the house to the kitchen.

'I hope it's not too late, but I told Hugo I'd call in after dinner—' Jake stopped dead as he caught sight of the gathered family. 'Sorry, I didn't realise you had company.'

'Just family,' Ellen said warmly. 'Jake, you remember everyone?'

Jake's eyes found Lisette's across the room, and that same electric awareness shot through her. Jake looked different tonight—his hair still damp from a recent shower, wearing jeans and a button-down shirt.

'I can come back another time,' Jake said, but Hugo was already waving him out to the veranda.

'Nonsense. Come in, we'll go to my office to look at the contract we discussed, and then you can join us for dessert. I'm pretty sure I smelled apple pie before.'

Jake entered reluctantly, glancing at Lisette before he turned his attention to Hugo. They moved down the hallway, their voices low and professional, but Lisette couldn't help watching them.

'You're staring,' Sarah murmured beside her.

Lisette jumped. 'I'm not.'

'You absolutely are.' Sarah grinned. 'And he's been glancing at you ever since he walked in with your mum. Whatever's happened between you two, it's not just about the farm sale.'

'Nothing's happened,' Lisette protested.

'Uh-huh.' Sarah's tone made it clear she didn't believe a word of it. 'For what it's worth, Jake's a good man. Loyal, hardworking, passionate about the things he cares about. And he's been carrying a torch for you for a long time, which is incredibly romantic.'

'You think?' Lisette tried to sound disinterested rather than intrigued.

'Everyone knows it. Well, everyone except apparently you and possibly Jake himself.' Sarah nudged her gently.

Before Lisette could respond, Jake and Dad came out of the study.

'Well, thank you for seeing me,' Jake said. 'Sounds like you've got a lot to talk about. I won't stay.'

'Please, stay for dessert,' Ellen urged.

'I appreciate it, but I really should get going.'

'Well, let me cut you a piece of pie to take home. You live by yourself now, don't you?'

Jake nodded, and then his eyes met Lisette's and held while Ellen hurried to the kitchen. She was soon back with a piece of pie wrapped in foil.

'Thank you, Ellen. That's very kind of you,' he said as he headed for the door. Lisette followed him.

'Jake, wait.'

He turned, with a wide smile.

'I wanted to talk to you,' she said quickly, before she could lose her nerve. 'To tell you how much I enjoy spending time with you. I'm staying in Duckinwilla. Becoming Julien's partner in the store. Investing in the family farm trust, if—hopefully Dad agrees.'

Jake's eyes widened. 'You're staying?'

'If...'

'If what?'

Lisette took a breath, gathering her courage. 'If certain people might be willing to give me a second chance at things I was too young and stupid to appreciate the first time around.'

Jake smiled—really smiled—Lisette felt her heart lift, a flutter of warmth rising inside.

'I think,' Jake said slowly, 'that certain people might be amenable to that possibility. Provided said person understood that this time, there'd be no running. No disappearing to Melbourne the moment things got too hard.'

'No running,' Lisette agreed. 'I'm done running.'

'Good.' Jake stepped closer, close enough that she had to tilt her head back to maintain eye contact. 'Because Duckinwilla's better with you in it. The store's better with you in it. And to be honest, I'm better with you in my life too.'

'Jake Morrison,' Lisette said softly, 'did you just admit to having feelings?'

'Don't let it go to your head.' But he was smiling, and so was she, and when he reached out to tuck a strand of hair behind her ear, Lisette didn't pull away.

'I should get back inside,' she said, not moving.

'You should,' Jake agreed, not stepping back. 'There's apple pie in there.'

'My family will be watching through the window.'

'Undoubtedly.'

'They'll gossip about this for weeks.'

'Months, more likely.'

'I don't care,' Lisette realised with surprise. 'Let them watch. Let them gossip. Let the whole town know that Lisette Johnson is staying in Duckinwilla and could be very interested in a boy she should have noticed a long time ago.'

'I'm not a boy anymore,' Jake pointed out.

'No,' Lisette agreed, very aware of Jake's closeness and the warmth radiating from him. The way her heart was racing had nothing to do with the night's events. 'No, you're definitely not.'

'Have dinner with me again,' Jake said abruptly. 'Tomorrow night. Somewhere we can talk without your entire family eavesdropping.'

'Is this a date?'

'If you want it to be.' Jake's confidence

wavered slightly, and Lisette caught a glimpse of the seventeen-year-old boy who'd stammered through his feelings on graduation night. 'Or it could just be two old friends catching up again. Your call.'

'It's a date,' Lisette said firmly. 'Seven o'clock?'

'I'll pick you up at six-thirty. Wear something comfortable—I have plans that don't involve the pub.'

'Mysterious. I like it.'

Jake grinned, his boyish charm making her heart beat even faster. 'Good. Because Lisette Johnson, I've waited a long time for this. I'm not about to waste it on predictable.'

He walked his ute with a confidence that made Lisette's stomach flutter. She stood on the veranda watching him drive away, very aware that behind her, at least five family members were definitely pressed against the windows.

She turned to face them, finding exactly the scene she'd expected—Charlotte and Amelia staring, Sarah trying to look casual while clearly having watched every moment, Julien grinning like Christmas had come early.

'Not one word,' Lisette warned, walking back inside.

'Wouldn't dream of it,' Charlotte said innocently. 'Though I will say Jake Morrison is very tidy.'

'And apparently still carries a torch,' Amelia added.

'Which you're finally noticing,' Oli finished.

Lisette groaned. 'This is why I left.'

'No,' Sarah said gently. 'You left because you were scared. But you're not scared anymore, are you?'

Lisette thought about the conversation inside—her announcement about staying, about investing in the family trust, about choosing Duckinwilla over Melbourne. About Jake on the veranda, offering her a second chance at something she'd been too young to appreciate.

'No,' she said finally. 'I'm not scared anymore. Terrified, maybe. But not scared.'

'Good,' Ellen said, appearing from the kitchen with a plate of apple pie and cream in each hand. 'Because life's too short to let fear take over. I should know—your father and I have been letting fear control us for months now. Maybe it's time we all stopped running from the hard things and started running toward them instead.'

She looked at Hugo, who'd been listening from his chair at the head of the table.

'We'll talk to the financial adviser first thing tomorrow,' he said. 'About the trust, about Oli's proposal, about all of it. No promises, but we'll look at the numbers properly.'

Sarah wrapped her arms around Oli, and Jett—who'd been playing quietly with his LEGO in the corner—looked up with a six-year-old's perfect intuition that something important had been said.

'Does this mean we get to stay on the farm, Grandpa?' he asked Hugo.

'Maybe, little man,' Hugo replied, his voice rough with emotion. 'Maybe we all get to stay, just in different ways.'

As the evening drew to a close, Lisette stood at the kitchen window, looking out over the cane stalks silvery in the moonlight.

This was home. Dad appeared beside her, two mugs of tea in his hands. He offered one to her.

'You're really staying here, because if—'

'I'm staying because I want to,' Lisette interrupted. 'Because being here, I've felt more myself than I have in years. Because the store matters, the farm matters, this whole crazy community matters.' She smiled at him. 'And because apparently I have unfinished business with a stock and station agent who's been carrying a torch for me.'

Dad laughed. 'About time you noticed Jake. The rest of us have been waiting for you to wake up and realise what you walked away from.'

'I was nineteen and stupid.'

'You were nineteen and scared,' her father corrected. 'You had all that drama with Brett, and I think more than anything, you wanted to move away from family to sort yourself out, away from our influence, away from where you always knew we would forgive. There's a difference. And now you're back, older and wiser and ready to actually build something instead of just running away from it. Finding the right person changes everything, Lis. It makes you braver somehow. Makes you want to take risks you'd never consider on your own.'

'Is that what this is? Taking a risk on Jake?'

'Taking a risk on yourself,' Dad replied. 'On the life you actually want instead of the life you thought you were supposed to want. Jake's just the bonus.'

They stood quietly side by side, looking out at the silvery cane fields until Dad put his arm around her shoulder. 'We're proud of you, Lis. And it makes your Mum and me happy to see you smiling. To see you talking to Char and Melie with no harsh words between you anymore.'

Lisette leaned into him slightly. 'You know, Dad, I used to think coming home would mean giving up on my dreams.' She paused, listening to the sounds of her family drifting from inside—laughter, the clatter of dishes, Mum's voice calling out something she couldn't quite make out. 'But standing here tonight, with all of you... I think I'm finally figuring out what those dreams actually were.'

Chapter 12

Jake picked Lisette up at six-thirty, driving a ute that was cleaner than she'd expected and smelling faintly of the same soap-and-sun scent she remembered from their encounter at the store. He'd made an effort—pressed jeans, a blue shirt that brought out his eyes, boots that weren't caked in paddock mud.

'You look nervous,' Lisette observed as they pulled away from the store, where she'd been finishing up the day's accounts.

'Do I?' Jake's hands tightened on the steering wheel. 'Probably because I've dreamed about this moment for six years, and I'm terrified of stuffing it up.'

The honesty in his words made Lisette's heart twist. 'Where are we going?'

'You'll see.' Jake smiled, some of his confidence returning. 'I promised you unpredictable.'

They drove out of town, past familiar

landmarks that Lisette had spent years trying to forget—the old swimming hole where they'd spent summer afternoons, the lookout where she'd gone to think when life felt too small, the turn-off to Jake's family property. When he took that turn, Lisette raised an eyebrow.

'Taking me home to meet your parents on our first date? Bit presumptuous, Morrison.'

Jake laughed. 'Mum and Dad are in Toowoomba visiting my sister. The house is empty, which means we can actually have a conversation without the entire district knowing about it by morning.'

He pulled up in front of a weatherboard homestead that was larger and more modern than Lisette remembered. The Morrison property had always been smaller than the Johnson farm, but what it lacked in size it made up for in presentation. The gardens were immaculate, the fences all painted, the machinery sheds in perfect order.

'You've made improvements,' Lisette said as Jake led her around to the back veranda.

'Six years' worth.' Jake gestured to a table set with candles, wine glasses, and what appeared to be a professionally catered meal. 'I wasn't going to cook and risk poisoning you on our first date, so I may have called in a favour from the restaurant in Dunmora.'

'Impressive.' Lisette sat down, touched by the effort he'd made. 'Though I have to ask—have you been planning this since I left, or did you pull it together after last night?'

'Bit of both.' Jake poured wine, his hand steady despite his earlier admission of nerves. 'I've thought about what I'd say to you if you ever came back. What I'd do differently. Then you showed up and I panicked and said all the wrong things anyway.'

'You said some right things too,' Lisette admitted. 'Hard things, but right. I needed to hear them.'

They ate looking over paddocks that rolled away towards the Duckinwilla ranges, the sky turning shades of pink and gold as the sun dipped below the hills. The food was excellent, but Lisette barely tasted it, too aware of Jake across from her—the way he moved, the way he listened, the way he'd grown into himself in the years she'd been gone.

'Tell me about Melbourne,' Jake said eventually. 'What you did there, why you're really leaving it behind.'

Lisette considered lying, giving him the polished version she'd perfected for family questions. But something about tonight—the isolation, the honesty, the years of unfinished business between them—made her honest.

'I went to Melbourne because I was scared,' she said finally. 'Scared of being trapped, of becoming invisible, of turning into just another farmer's daughter in a town where everyone already knew my story. I thought if I could get away, reinvent myself somewhere nobody knew me, I'd figure out who I was supposed to be.'

'And did you?'

'I figured out who I wasn't.' Lisette swirled her wine, watching the liquid catch the candlelight. 'I built this perfect city life— fabulous job, nice apartment, friends who knew all the right restaurants. On paper, I was exactly who nineteen-year-old Lisette dreamed of becoming.'

'But?'

'But it was exhausting. Maintaining this

façade of someone sophisticated and cosmopolitan, someone who'd left her roots behind and moved on to bigger things. I was lonely, Jake. Surrounded by people but completely alone, because none of them knew the real me. The me who grew up feeding cattle and driving tractors and thinking the Duckinwilla Show was the social event of the year.'

Jake reached across the table, his fingers brushing hers. 'Why didn't you come back sooner?'

'Pride, mostly. I'd made such a production of leaving, of proving I was destined for greater things. Coming back would have felt like admitting failure.' Lisette turned her hand over, letting their fingers intertwine. 'Especially coming back to face the boy I'd hurt on the way out.'

'I wasn't a boy, Lis. I was seventeen and stupid enough to confess feelings to a girl who'd made it very clear one day she would leave the valley.'

'It took me two years to save up, but I was cruel to you,' Lisette said quietly. 'That night, what I said about needing to find myself somewhere that wasn't Duckinwilla—'

'Was honest,' Jake interrupted. 'It hurt like hell, but you were honest about what you wanted. I respected that, even if I hated it.'

'And now?' Lisette looked up, meeting his eyes. 'What do you want now?'

Jake was quiet for a long moment, his thumb tracing patterns on her hand. When he spoke, his voice was rough with emotion.

'I want what I've always wanted. You. Here, in Duckinwilla, building a life that matters. But I'm not seventeen anymore, Lis. I'm not going to beg you to stay or make promises about changing your mind. If you're back, you're back because it's what you want, not because I convinced you.'

'I'm back because it's what I want,' Lisette confirmed. 'Because this week, working in the store, reconnecting with family, arguing with you about things that actually matter—I've felt more alive than I have in years. Melbourne was safe and predictable and slowly suffocating me. This is messy and complicated and exactly where I'm supposed to be.'

'Even though everyone will have opinions

about us? About what we're doing, whether it'll last, how fast we're moving?'

Lisette laughed. 'Especially because of that. Let them talk. Let them speculate. I'm done caring what people think about my choices.'

Jake grinned, that boyish charm breaking through again. 'Good. Because Lisette Johnson, I plan on giving them plenty to talk about.'

He stood up, pulling her with him, and before Lisette could ask what he was doing, he was kissing her—properly kissing her, with pent-up longing behind it. She melted into him, hands fisting in his shirt, finally allowing herself to feel what she'd been suppressing since he'd walked into the store.

When they finally broke apart, both breathing hard, Jake rested his forehead against hers.

'I've wanted to do that since Year Eleven chemistry,' he admitted.

'You should have,' Lisette replied. 'Would have saved us both years of waiting.'

'Some things are worth waiting for.' Jake pulled back slightly, studying her face in the candlelight. 'But I'm not waiting anymore. Fair warning—I'm not good at slow. I'm not good at casual. If we're doing this, I'm all in.'

'Good,' Lisette said firmly. 'Because I spent too long doing casual and careful and keeping my options open. I'm ready for all in.'

They spent the rest of the evening on Jake's veranda, talking between kisses. Jake told her about the years after she'd left, about building up the family stock and station agency business, about watching other people leave while he chose to stay and invest in the community she'd abandoned.

'What about the farm?' Jake asked eventually. 'The family trust, Oli's plan to take over—do you think your parents will agree?'

'I don't know,' Lisette admitted. 'But I hope so. Oli deserves the chance to prove himself, and Dad deserves to retire without feeling like he's destroyed the family legacy.'

'And if it doesn't work out? If the trust falls through and the sale goes ahead?'

'Then we'll deal with it,' Lisette said. 'Together. All of us. Because that's what families do—they adapt, they survive, they find new ways to stay connected even when circumstances change.'

Jake pulled her closer, and Lisette rested her head against his shoulder, feeling the steady beat of his heart beneath her ear. In the distance, cattle called to each other across the paddocks, the sound as familiar as her own breathing.

'Thank you,' she said quietly.

'For what?'

'For waiting. For still being here when I finally got smart enough to come back. For giving me a second chance at something I was too young and stupid to appreciate the first time.'

'Always,' Jake replied simply. 'I'd wait another six years if that's what it took.'

'It won't take six years,' Lisette promised. 'In fact, it won't take six days. I'm here, Jake. I'm staying. And I'm not running anymore.'

Chapter 13

The family meeting two weeks later was very different from the last one. Less tension, more hope, although the underlying anxiety remained. They gathered this time at *Grandmère* and Papa's homestead, all six Johnson siblings plus partners, Hugo and Ellen, and the elderly grandparents whose wisdom had shaped three generations.

Lisette arrived with Jake, whose hand she held without self-consciousness or apology. The knowing looks from her siblings were worth ignoring for the comfort of his presence beside her.

'Right,' Hugo said once everyone was settled. 'Mum and I have been doing a lot of thinking and a lot of number-crunching over the past two weeks. We've met with the financial adviser, the bank, and a lawyer who specialises in family trusts.'

The room held its collective breath.

'We've decided,' Ellen continued, reaching

for Hugo's hand, 'to accept your offer. We're going to form a family trust, with Oli as the primary operator and all of you as investors.'

The tension shattered into pure relief and excitement. Oli's face crumpled as Sarah wrapped her arms around him. Charlotte burst into tears. Guy was grinning, and Amelia actually cheered. Lisette threw her arms around Jake and kissed him.

'There are conditions,' Hugo said loudly, cutting through the celebration. 'Lots of them. The trust structure will protect everyone's investment but also limit individual exposure. Oli will have operational control, but major decisions require family consensus. We're selling this house to buy into our retirement unit at Pacific Palms, and *Grandmère* and Papa will still be moving as planned—'

'Already packed,' Papa interjected. 'Sunset Manor, here we come.'

'—and we're still taking three months to visit France before we settle,' *Grandmère* added. 'Some things don't change just because the farm stays in the family.'

'The farm stays in the family,' Oli repeated,

as if testing the words. 'The farm actually stays in the family.'

'Yes,' Hugo said, his voice thick. 'The farm stays. And maybe, just maybe, your grandfather and I can grow old knowing we didn't fail you children after all.'

'You never failed us,' Charlotte said fiercely. 'Not for one second. You gave us roots and wings, and now we're choosing to use those wings to come back to our roots.'

'Very poetic,' Julien teased, but his eyes were glistening with moisture.

The conversations that followed were practical: solicitors to contact, documents to sign, a timeline for the sale to be cancelled, and the trust to be established. Oli outlined his vision for the farm's future with a passion that left no doubt about his commitment. Guy offered his consulting services pro bono. Julien and Lisette discussed expanding the store's departments to support the new direction of the farm. Charlotte sat there with a hand on her stomach and a happy smile.

Through it all, Lisette felt Jake's hand in hers. When she looked around the room—at her siblings planning their shared future, at her parents finally allowing themselves to believe retirement didn't mean failure, at *Grandmère* and Papa watching their legacy continue into another generation—happiness almost overwhelmed her.

The happiness of a messy, complicated, beautiful reality of caring about the family she loved. She turned and looked up at Jake.

'You alright?' he murmured, his breath warm against her ear.

'Perfect,' Lisette replied. 'I'm absolutely perfect.'

Chapter 14

Three months later, Lisette stood in Johnson's General Store at six-thirty in the morning, preparing for the day's opening. She'd settled seamlessly into life back in Duckinwilla, happy with the rhythm of small-town life.

The store was thriving under her and Julien's partnership. They'd expanded the online presence, secured new suppliers, and implemented systems that kept the personal touch that made rural retail work. Customers who'd been sceptical of the "city sister" had been won over by her genuine interest in their lives and her absolute refusal to pretend she was anything other than a Johnson daughter who'd finally come home.

As she turned the coffee machine on, the doorbell chimed, and Lisette looked up. Jake carried two takeaway coffees and two fresh pastries from the bakery up the street and wore the smile that still made her stomach flip.

'Morning, beautiful, I knew your machine

wouldn't have warmed up yet,' he said, kissing her with the closeness of three months of steady courtship. 'And I thought you might need fuel before Mrs Patterson arrives demanding her arthritis liniment and forty-five minutes of conversation.'

'You're a lifesaver.' Lisette accepted the coffee gratefully. 'Though I'm fairly certain Mrs Patterson just comes in to gather intelligence on our relationship for sharing with the rest of the district.'

'Undoubtedly, we're famous in the valley.' Jake leaned against the counter, his eyes full of love. 'Speaking of our relationship, I've been thinking.'

'Dangerous habit.'

'Shush. I've been thinking that three months is long enough for dating. I know what I want, Lis. I've known since we were in high school together, and the last three months have only confirmed it.'

Lisette's heart started racing. 'Jake...'

'I'm not proposing,' he said quickly. 'Not yet, anyway. But I am asking if you'd consider moving in with me. Not because it's convenient or practical, but because I hate spending nights apart. Because I want to wake up with you every morning and fall asleep with you every night. Because my house is too big and too quiet without you in it.'

'But I live above the store,' Lisette pointed out, though her pulse was hammering.

'I know. And if you want to keep your space, that's fine. But I thought maybe you might want a proper home with a garden. Well, there was a garden before Mum and Dad moved.' He hesitated and held her eyes with his. 'But also, with a guy who's been in love with you since he was seventeen.'

Lisette set down her coffee carefully. Three months ago—well, even three weeks ago—she would have said it was too soon, too fast, too much. But standing in the store that she loved managing, in the town that had always been home, looking at the man who'd waited for her to figure out what mattered...

'Yes,' she said. 'Yes, to all of it. The house, the garden, the man who's been patiently waiting for me to pull my head out of the sand and realise what I had right in front of me.'

Jake's whoop of joy startled her into laughter. He grabbed her, spinning her around the store with complete disregard for the stacked merchandise and the impending arrival of customers.

'We're doing this,' he said when he finally set her down. 'Actually doing this. Building a life together in Duckinwilla.'

'We are,' Lisette confirmed, framing his face with her hands. 'And Jake? I'm not scared anymore. I'm not running. This is exactly where I want to be.'

They were still kissing when Mrs Patterson arrived at seven o'clock sharp, tapping on the glass door with her walking stick and wearing an expression of supreme satisfaction.

'About bloody time,' she announced to absolutely no one as Lisette hurried to turn the sign to open. 'The whole district's been waiting for you two to get your act together. Now, do you have my liniment, or am I going to have to listen to how Jake Morrison proposed before I can ease my aching joints?'

'He didn't propose,' Lisette corrected, though she was grinning. 'He asked me to move in with him.'

'Same difference these days.' Mrs Patterson held her hand out for the liniment that Lisette took off the shelf. 'Mark my words, you'll be engaged by Christmas and married by next June. I've seen enough courting in my eighty-three years to know when two people are heading for the altar.'

'I'll take that bet,' Jake called from behind the counter, where he was helping unpack the morning's delivery. 'Christmas seems awfully soon.'

'Sooner than you think, boy.' Mrs Patterson headed for the door, then paused. 'For what it's worth, I'm glad you're back, Lisette. Town's better with you in it. And that brother of yours needs someone to keep him organised.'

'I heard that,' Julien said, emerging from the back office with a stack of paperwork.

'You were meant to.' Mrs Patterson left with a wave, no doubt already composing the morning's gossip bulletin in her head.

'And that,' Julien said cheerfully, 'is why I love small-town life. Absolute zero privacy, but at least everyone cares enough to be nosy.'

'Says the man about to leave on a European tour,' Lisette retorted. 'How's Emily?'

'Stressed about the packing, excited about Italy, and absolutely certain we're doing the right thing by expanding the store's online presence before we leave for six months.' Julien smiled at his sister. 'Thanks for this, Lis. For staying. For becoming my partner. For actually caring about making this work.'

'Thanks for letting me,' Lisette replied. 'For giving me a place to come home to.'

The door chimed again—Sarah arriving to collect supplies for the surgery, followed by Bill Murphy needing feed, then young Amy Grant picking up her mother's order. The morning rush built steadily, and Lisette fell into the rhythm of rural retail with the ease of someone who'd finally found her place.

At lunchtime, when the store quieted, she took her sandwich to the front step and sat in the winter sun, looking down Duckinwilla's main street. The bakery, the pub, and the agency where Jake spent his working day. The post office where Mrs Grant reigned supreme. The school where Charlotte taught, the surgery where Sarah now worked, and the pre-school where Amelia had started her traineeship.

This was her community now. Not the anonymous city where she'd hidden for three years, but this small, nosy, complicated collection of people who knew her history and cared about her future. Who'd welcomed her back without making her grovel. Who'd given her the gift of belonging.

Her phone buzzed with a text from Charlotte: **Family dinner Sunday. Grandies back from France.** *Grandmère* **wants to show off photos. Mandatory attendance. Bring Jake.**

Lisette smiled, typing back: **We'll be there. And Char? Thank you. For organising that first meeting. For pushing us to fight for the farm. For reminding us what matters.**

The reply came quickly: **That's what big sisters do. Even when we're technically the middle child. Love you.**

'Love you too,' Lisette murmured to her phone, to the empty street, to the whole ridiculous town that had become her home again.

Jake appeared around the corner, walking from his office with that long-legged stride she'd come to love. He spotted her on the step and grinned, changing course to join her.

'Fancy seeing you here,' he said, sitting close enough that their shoulders touched.

'Just enjoying the view,' Lisette replied.

'The view of the main street?' Jake teased.

'The view of my life,' Lisette corrected. 'The one I once thought I didn't want, that turned out to be exactly what I did.'

Jake wrapped an arm around her shoulders, and they sat together in comfortable silence as Duckinwilla went about its business. In the distance, the ranges rose blue against the late winter sky, marking the boundaries of the valley that meant so much to her family.

She'd left this place searching for herself and spent three years away from what mattered. But sometimes, she'd learned, you had to leave home to understand what home and family really meant.

And sometimes—just sometimes—the boy you'd left behind grew into the man who'd been waiting for you to come home all along.

'What are you thinking?' Jake asked softly.

Lisette turned to kiss him, slow and sweet and full of promise. 'I'm thinking,' she said against his lips, 'that Mrs Patterson was right. We'll probably be engaged by Christmas.'

'And married by June?' Jake's eyes crinkled with amusement.

'Don't push your luck, Morrison.'

'Wouldn't dream of it,' Jake replied. 'I've got all the time in the world now that you're not going anywhere.'

'Nowhere,' Lisette agreed. 'Except possibly to the farm on Sunday for dinner, to your place tonight after work, and eventually—soon—down an aisle toward a man who was patient enough not to give up as he waited for me to grow up and come home.'

'Sounds perfect to me.' Jake stood, pulling her with him. 'Now come on—I believe you have a store to run and a community to serve. And I have properties to inspect and gossip to collect. Standard Thursday in Duckinwilla.'

'Standard Thursday,' Lisette echoed, but she was smiling as she followed him back inside.

Because there was nothing standard about

any of it—not the thought of family that had brought her home, not the farm trust that had saved their legacy, not the romance that had been waiting since high school to finally begin. This was her reality.

And for the first time, Lisette Johnson wasn't running from it.

She was running towards it—toward home and family, towards love, to live the life she'd been meant to live all along.

All together now, just as it should be.

Epilogue

The Christmas heat shimmered over the Duckinwilla Valley as Charlotte navigated her sedan carefully up the farm drive, three-month-old Hugh Robert—named for his grandfather and great-grandfather—sleeping peacefully in his capsule. Beside her, Greg was reading aloud from a list on his phone—presents packed, bottles sterilised, nappies counted twice, every eventuality prepared for.

'We're only going to the farm,' Charlotte reminded him gently. 'Not emigrating to France.'

'First Christmas with the baby,' Greg replied, as if that explained everything. 'Your mum will have opinions about feeding schedules. Your sisters will have advice. And God knows what chaos will erupt with your entire family gathered. My parents will sit there in shock, like they usually do.'

'That's because you're an only child.'

Charlotte smiled. *Her entire family*. Six

months ago, that phrase had been stressful for all of them—the impending sale of the farm, *Grandmère* and Papa's move to aged care, Lisette's return, the scattering of a family that had been rooted in this valley for three generations. Now it meant something different. Something precious and hard-won and absolutely worth fighting for.

The farmhouse rose before them, transformed by fresh paint and new guttering that Oli had insisted on before the summer storms. The gardens burst with colour—Ellen's work, replanted with native species that could survive the Queensland heat without constant attention. Solar panels gleamed on the machinery shed roof, part of his ongoing modernisation program.

Cars already crowded the yard. Julien's sedan and Guy's ute were parked next to Amelia's practical SUV. And there, slightly apart, Jake Morrison's truck—because apparently he came with Lisette now, a package deal that still made Charlotte smile every time she thought about it.

'Ready?' Greg asked, already unbuckling his seatbelt.

'Ready,' Charlotte confirmed, though she paused to look out over the paddocks one more time. The cane had been harvested weeks ago, leaving ratoon stubble that would green up with the summer rains. The cattle grazed contentedly in the creek paddock. And in the distance, she could see the new fence line that marked the boundary of what was now officially 'Johnson Family Trust Property'.

They'd done it. Against all odds, they'd actually pulled it off.

Inside, the house buzzed with the familiar chaos of a Johnson gathering. Oli and Sarah were in the kitchen with Ellen, arguing good-naturedly about whether the pavlova needed more fruit or if it should be left alone. Julien and Emily sat at the dining table with Hugo, discussing the store's expansion plans and laughing about Mrs Patterson's latest attempts to organise everyone's lives. Amelia and Daniel were on the floor with seven-year-old Jett, building what appeared to be a LEGO recreation of the farm.

And in the corner, Lisette and Jake were wrapped around each other on the sofa, looking so thoroughly comfortable together that

Charlotte wondered how she'd ever thought they wouldn't work out.

'There's my namesake,' Hugo announced, spotting baby Hugh in Charlotte's arms. 'Let me see him properly.'

Charlotte handed over her son, watching her father's face transform as he cradled two-month-old Hugh against his chest. This was what they'd fought for, she realised. Not just the land or the legacy, but this—the ability for three generations to gather under one roof, connected by blood and love and stubborn determination to preserve what mattered.

'How's retirement treating you, Dad?' Guy asked, appearing from the veranda with Elena. 'You look relaxed.'

'I look old,' Hugo corrected, but he was smiling. 'Though I have to admit, watching Oli run this place has been... enlightening. Turns out there are better ways to do things than the ways I've always done them.'

'Careful, Dad,' Oli called from the kitchen. 'That almost sounded like a compliment.'

'Don't let it go to your head,' Hugo replied, but his pride was evident. 'Though I will say the organic certification application looks solid. And the agritourism plan is way more comprehensive than I expected.'

'Learned from the best,' Oli said simply, and Charlotte saw her father's eyes shimmer with emotion.

'Right,' Ellen announced, emerging from the kitchen with Sarah. 'Lunch is ready. Everyone outside—it's too hot to eat indoors, and besides, *Grandmère* and Papa will be here any minute.'

They moved to the back veranda, where tables had been pushed together to accommodate the growing family. The view stretched away towards the ranges, unchanged and perfect, a vista that had watched over countless family gatherings and would watch over countless more.

Grandmère and Papa arrived in their new car—one of the concessions to aged living that Hugo had insisted on—driven by a young man from Sunset Manor who'd apparently become their designated chauffeur. Respectively. They moved more slowly than Charlotte remembered, but their spirits were undimmed.

'There are my grandchildren,' *Grandmère* announced, accepting hugs from everyone. 'And my two great-grandsons! Hugo, let me see him.'

Baby Hugh was passed around like a precious parcel, each family member taking their turn to coo over his tiny features and declare him the most beautiful baby ever born. Even Jake, who Charlotte suspected knew absolutely nothing about babies, held him with surprising ease while Lisette looked on with an expression that suggested Mrs Patterson's Christmas wedding prediction might not be far off.

'Where's Jett?' Papa asked, settling into his chair. 'I brought something for him.'

'LEGO farm set.' Jett appeared on cue. 'Mum said you had a surprise.'

'Better than LEGO,' Papa replied, pulling a carefully wrapped package from his bag. 'Open it carefully.'

The boy tore into the paper with seven-year-old enthusiasm, revealing a wooden box. Inside, nested in tissue paper, was a model farm— buildings, animals, fences, all carved from timber with exquisite detail.

'I made it,' Papa said quietly. 'Spent three

months in the workshop at Sunset Manor after we came home from France, driving the other residents mad with sawdust. It's this farm, or as close as I could remember. The house like it was when we built it. The sheds your father added. The creek paddock where your *Grandmère* and I used to walk on Sunday evenings.'

Jett stared at the model with an awe that suggested he understood, even at seven, that this was something precious beyond measure.

'It's our farm,' he breathed. 'It's exactly our farm.'

'It's your farm now,' Papa corrected. 'Yours and Oli's and Mum's and someday your little brother's or sister's. But it started with me and *Grandmère*, building something from nothing. And now you get to be part of that story.'

'Best present ever,' Jett declared, carefully lifting out the model barn. 'Can we put it in my room?'

Oli and Sarah exchanged a smile. The homestead had stayed a family home. Hugo and Ellen had their unit at Pacific Palms. *Grandmère* and Papa had their unit at Sunset Manor. But the farm itself belonged to the next generation, and the generation after that.

'Course you can, mate,' Oli said, ruffling his son's hair. 'That's your family history. You should see it every day.'

Lunch was served—plates passed around, conversations overlapped, and laughter punctuated debates about everything from cricket scores to the best way to grow tomatoes. Baby Hugh woke and was fed by Charlotte while everyone oohed and aahed at how beautiful he was. Jett showed everyone who'd listen how each piece of Papa's model fit together.

'I have an announcement,' Amelia said when the meal had wound down and everyone was waiting for the pavlova. 'Daniel and I are buying a house. The place we've been renting—the old Henderson cottage.'

The table erupted in excitement and questions.

'You're buying it?' Ellen's face lit up. 'Oh, that's wonderful!'

'We fell in love with it,' Amelia said, reaching for Daniel's hand. 'And when Mrs Henderson said they were ready to sell, we couldn't let it go. Daniel's been offered an IT position at the new medical centre they're building in town, so we could afford it.'

'That cottage is perfect for you two,' Charlotte said warmly.

'It needs work,' Daniel admitted with a grin, 'but it's ours.'

Charlotte blinked away tears. Six months ago, they'd been facing the dissolution of everything their family had built. Now they were expanding, putting down roots, choosing to stay when they could have left.

'That makes six of us,' Julien observed. 'Five out of six in our own places. Not bad for a family that was supposedly scattering to the winds.'

'Who's the sixth?' young Jett asked, looking around in confusion.

'Us,' Guy said quietly. 'Elena and I are still renting.'

An awkward silence fell over the table. The Brazilian option—Elena's family's farm, the opportunity that had nearly pulled Guy away from Australia entirely—hung unspoken between them.

'But,' Elena said, speaking up for the first

time, 'we are thinking about alternatives. My family would like to expand their operations to Australia. Import Brazilian coffee, establish partnerships with local farms. Guy has been consulting on the feasibility.'

'Meaning?' Charlotte prompted.

'Meaning we might be here more than you think,' Guy said, smiling at his wife. 'If the business works out, we'd split our time—six months here, six months in Brazil. Best of both worlds.'

'Compromises all around,' Hugo observed. 'Good to see. Figuring out how everyone gets what they need, even when those needs seem contradictory.'

'Speaking of compromises,' Lisette said, exchanging glances with Jake, 'we have news too. Jake and I are engaged.' She held up her left hand where a new diamond ring sparkled.

Another eruption, this one accompanied by shrieks from Charlotte and Amelia, groans from the brothers about how they'd have to get used to Jake being officially family, and knowing looks from literally everyone present.

'Mrs Patterson wins the betting pool,' Ellen

announced. 'She said Christmas.'

'You had a betting pool about my engagement?' Lisette demanded.

'The whole town had a betting pool,' Sarah corrected. 'Mrs Grant at the post office was coordinating it. I think the proceeds are going to the new playground fund.'

'At least our relationship is supporting community infrastructure,' Jake said dryly, though his arm around Lisette suggested he couldn't care less what the town thought.

'When's the wedding?' Charlotte asked.

'June,' Lisette replied. 'Next year, at the homestead, if Oli and Sarah will let us use the property.'

'Of course,' Sarah said immediately. 'It would be an honour.'

The afternoon drifted on in that timeless way of perfect summer days—while baby Hugh slept peacefully in various family members' arms.

Charlotte stood at the veranda railing, looking out over the farm that had nearly been lost, now saved by a combination of love and determination.

'Worth fighting for?' Oli appeared beside

her, holding baby Hugh.

'Absolutely,' Charlotte replied. 'Though I have to ask—are you terrified? Taking on all this responsibility?'

'Every day,' Oli admitted. 'But the good kind of terrified. The kind that means you care enough to worry about doing it right.' He looked down at his nephew. 'That's what this is all about, isn't it? Making sure the next generation has something worth inheriting.'

'And if they don't want it? If Jett or Hugh or whoever comes next decides farming isn't for them?'

'Then we adapt,' Oli said simply. 'Like we always have. Papa left France and started over. Dad built on what Papa created. Now it's my turn. And someday, it'll be their turn—whatever that looks like.'

Grandmère joined them, moving slowly but with purpose. 'Are you two being philosophical without me?'

'Just contemplating the future of the Johnson legacy,' Charlotte said, making room for her grandmother.

'The legacy isn't the land or the farm,'

Grandmère said firmly. 'It never has been. The legacy is this—' she gestured to the veranda full of family, arguing and laughing and simply being together. 'The legacy is knowing that no matter what happens, family figures it out together. That's what we built here. And that's what will continue.'

'No pressure then,' Oli joked.

'Enormous pressure,' *Grandmère* corrected. 'But you're managing beautifully. All of you. Even you, Lisette,' she called over her shoulder, 'though it took you long enough to figure out where you belonged.'

'Better late than never,' Lisette replied, snuggled against Jake on the sofa.

Hugo stood up, clearing his throat in the way that meant he had something to say. The family quietened, turning their attention to him.

'I want to propose a toast,' he began, his voice rough with emotion. 'Six months ago, Ellen and I thought selling the farm was our only option. We thought we were failing you children, failing the legacy Papa and *Grandmère* built, failing ourselves. But you proved us wrong. You fought for this place when we were too tired to fight for it ourselves. You saw solutions where we saw only problems. And most importantly, you reminded us that family isn't about land. It's about adapting, compromising, and supporting each other through whatever comes.'

He raised his glass. 'So here's to the Johnson family—all of us, from Papa and *Grandmère* who started this adventure, to baby Hugh who represents the future we're building together. Here's to the farm that nearly got away and the children who refused to let it go. Here's to Christmas, to family, and to the next chapter of a story that's just beginning.'

'To family,' everyone chorused, glasses raised.

Charlotte clinked her glass against Greg's, then reached across to touch Amelia's, Julien's, Guy's, Oli's, and Lisette's. Her siblings, her family, her tribe. They'd fought and argued and nearly fallen apart, but in the end, they'd chosen each other. Chosen to stay, to invest, to build something together that none of them could build alone.

The afternoon faded into evening, the summer heat mellowing into the kind of golden light that made everything seem possible. Jett fell asleep with his head in Sarah's lap, the farm model carefully packed away for transport home. Baby Hugh fed and dozed and fed again, passed from family member to family member like the precious gift he was.

Grandmère and Papa said their goodbyes as the sun touched the ranges, their driver helping them into the car. Charlotte hugged them both, breathing in the familiar scents of lavender and Old Spice, memorising the feel of their arms around her.

'Thank you,' she whispered to *Grandmère*. 'For starting this. For giving us all something worth fighting for.'

'Thank Papa,' *Grandmère* replied. 'He's the one who started this adventure.'

'Best decision I ever made,' Papa said, overhearing. 'Well, second best. First best was marrying this woman—that gave you all the opportunity to have this life. That's my legacy. Not the land, not the farm.'

They drove away slowly, *Grandmère* waving from the passenger window like a departing queen. Charlotte watched until the car disappeared around the bend, then turned back to the house.

'Ready to head home?' Greg asked, baby Hugh sleeping in his arms.

'In a minute,' Charlotte said. 'I just want to remember this.'

She stood on the veranda steps, taking in the view one more time. The paddocks stretching towards the ranges. The machinery sheds that held three generations of farming history. The main house, where it had all started, was now freshly painted and gleaming in the evening light.

This was what home looked like. Not perfect, not unchanged, but alive and absolutely worth every fight they'd waged to preserve it.

Inside, she could hear Lisette laughing at something Jake said. Julien explaining something to Emily with his characteristic seriousness. Amelia and Daniel discussing paint colours for their new house. Guy and Elena planning their next trip between countries. Oli and Sarah collecting their sleeping son and putting him to bed.

Six Johnson siblings, six different lives, six

different versions of what it meant to be family. But all of them choosing, in their own ways, to stay connected to this place and to each other.

Charlotte walked to the car, settling Hugh into his capsule while Greg double-checked that they had everything they'd need for the drive home. Through the window, she could see her parents on the veranda, Ellen's head resting on Hugo's shoulder as they watched the last of the sunset paint the sky in shades of pink and gold.

They'd earned their rest, Charlotte thought. After forty years of carrying the worry of the farm as they brought up their children, they'd finally been able to pass it on to willing hands. Not perfect hands, not experienced hands, but hands that cared enough to try.

As they drove away, Charlotte looked back one more time at the farm that had nearly been lost and was now secured for another generation. At the family that had nearly scattered and was now choosing to stay close. At the legacy that had seemed so fragile and was now being strengthened by six different approaches to the same shared goal.

'What are you thinking?' Greg asked.

'I'm thinking,' Charlotte said softly, 'that home isn't a place you come from. It's a place you choose. And I'm glad we all chose this.'

The car crested the rise, and the farm disappeared from view behind them. But Charlotte carried it with her—in her heart, in her memories, in her son who would grow up knowing his roots and understanding his place in a story that stretched back three generations and forward into a future they were all building together.

All together now, just as it should be.

MERRY CHRISTMAS FROM THE JOHNSON FAMILY.

I hope you've enjoyed meeting the Johnson family in the Duckinwilla Days stories.

Stay posted for my next series, The Happy Outback Hotel.

Book 1, Outback Strangers, will be out in February 2026.

When three English friends—Amelia, Sophie, and Charlotte—arrive in the dusty outback town of Garnet Creek during their gap year, they expect nothing more than a quick stop at the campground attached to an abandoned hotel. What they don't expect is to find themselves completely charmed by a town that's barely changed in decades.

The once-thriving Garnet Creek Hotel now serves as a basic campground, and sitting around the campfire one evening, the girls dare to dream: what if they could transform this forgotten pub into the heart of the community again—a proper English-style pub where locals and travellers alike could gather?

Their dream seems impossible until a mysterious fellow traveller, elderly philanthropist Alex Morrison, makes them an offer they can't refuse. Suddenly, they own the pub and face the mammoth task of bringing it back to life

The locals, however, are suspicious and not ready to embrace change—especially not from a trio of English backpackers. The town council is hostile, and tensions run high as old wounds and pride clash with the arrival of new residents. When Amelia finds herself drawn to Jake Sullivan, the talented builder caught between his loyalty to the town and his growing feelings for her, everything becomes far more complicated.

Can three young women from halfway around the world turn doubt into acceptance and transform a struggling town? Or will the outback prove too harsh for their English dreams?

You can pre-order Book 1 in eBook:

https://books2read.com/u/mqJG0Z

and print:

https://annieseatonstore.ecwid.com/Outback-Strangers-p781674310

Also by Annie Seaton

Daughters of the Darling
From Across the Sea
Over the River
By the Billabong
Beneath Still Waters
Under Darling Skies

A Bec Whitfield Mystery
Bowen River
Shadows on the Shore
Storm Season

The Happy Outback Hotel (2026)
Outback Strangers
Outback Secrets
Outback Dreams
Outback Hearts
Outback Spirit
Outback Promise
Outback Horizon
Outback Silence
Outback Whispers
Outback Flame
Duckinwilla Days
Coming Home
Secrets and Surprises

Wishes and Whispers
Chasing Dreams
New Beginnings
All Together Now

Home to the Outback
Lucy
Angie
Jemima
Isabella
Porter Sisters Series
Kakadu Sunset
Daintree
Diamond Sky
Hidden Valley
Larapinta
Kakadu Dawn

Others
Whitsunday Dawn
Undara
Osprey Reef
East of Alice
One Summer in Tuscany
Four Seasons Short and Sweet
Follow the Sun
Ten Days in Paradise
Deadly Secrets
Adventures in Time
Silver Valley Witch
The Emerald Necklace

A Clever Christmas
Christmas with the Boss
Her Christmas Star
The Emerald Necklace

The Augathella Girls Series
Outback Roads
Outback Sky
Outback Escape
Outback Wind
Outback Dawn
Outback Moonlight
Outback Dust
Outback Hope
Boxed Sets
Augathella Girls 1-4
Augathella Girls 5-8

Augathella Short and Sweet Series
An Augathella Surprise
An Augathella Baby
An Augathella Spring
An Augathella Christmas
An Augathella Wedding
An Augathella Easter
An Augathella Masquerade Ball
Boxed Set
Augathella Short and Sweet 1-3
Augathella Short and Sweet 1-4

Sunshine Coast Series

Waiting for Ana
The Trouble with Jack
Healing His Heart
Sunshine Coast Boxed Set
The Richards Brothers Series
The Trouble with Paradise
Marry in Haste
Outback Sunrise
Richards Brothers Boxed Set
Bondi Beach Love Series
Beach House
Beach Music
Beach Walk
Beach Dreams
The House on the Hill Boxed Set

Second Chance Bay Series
Her Outback Playboy
Her Outback Protector
Her Outback Haven
Her Outback Paradise
Boxed Set
The McDougalls of Second Chance Bay

Love Across Time Series
Come Back to Me
Follow Me
Finding Home
The Threads that Bind
Boxed Set
Love Across Time 1-4

Bindarra Creek
Worth the Wait
Full Circle
Secrets of River Cottage
A Clever Christmas
A Place to Belong
Hearts in Harmony

Awards

2024: Finalist – Romantic suspense category, RUBY award for *From Across the Sea.*

2023: Winner - Long contemporary novel category, RUBY award for *Larapinta.*

2023: Finalist - Australian Romance Readers Awards for *Kakadu Dawn,* the sixth and final book in the Porter Sisters series.

2018 and 2020: Finalist - for the NZ KORU Award.

2017: Winner - Best Established Author of the Year 2017 AUSROM

2017: Winner - Author of the Year 2014 AUSROM
 Best Established Author, Ausrom Readers' Choice.

2016, 2017, 2018, 2019: Longlisted - Sisters in Crime Davitt Awards

2016: Finalist - Book of the Year, Long Romance, RWA Ruby Awards for *Kakadu Sunset*

2015: Winner - Best Established Author of the Year AUSROM

www.ingramcontent.com/pod-product-compliance
Lightning Source LLC
Chambersburg PA
CBHW060550190726
48283CB00003B/950